DEATH FROM HIGH PLACES

A 1920s MYSTERY

BENEDICT BROWN

COPYRIGHT

For my father, Kevin,
I hope you would have liked this book an awful lot.

CHAPTER ONE

When you spend five days a week studying, eating and sleeping in a school, you keep your mind focused on the weekend to come. Whoever invented boarding schools must have been some sort of evil genius – and most likely a teacher, as the two things so often go hand in hand. What crueller system is there than locking three hundred excitable boys in the same building and telling them to behave on pain of corporal punishment? It was not the life for me, and I was one of the lucky ones.

My three friends, William, Will and Billy, were full-time inmates. They didn't have weekends to look forward to, and barely went home during the holidays for that matter. But, as my grandfather lived close to Oakton Academy, and owned half of the county, I got to swan off every Friday afternoon for a brief jolt of freedom.

"Come along, Chrissy! Come along, boy!" Grandfather shouted from his Rolls Royce when he spotted me emerging from the school one sunny afternoon in June. He sounded like he was talking to his dog. "There are adventures to be had and chances to be seized. You'll never get anywhere in life by dawdling."

I tucked my weighty satchel under my arm and ran as fast as my stubby legs would carry me. Over the last two months, my grandfather, the Most Honourable Marquess of Edgington, Lord of Cranley Hall (to give him his full title) had changed beyond recognition. At the positively ancient age of seventy-five, he'd emerged from a decade-long seclusion determined to embrace life. I thought it was absolutely wonderful that an old chap like him could have such modern ideas about the world. I was less keen on the fact that he planned to drag me along with him into each new half-cocked scheme.

"I've got quite the weekend planned for us." His moustache bristled happily as I climbed alongside him into the luxurious backseat. Travelling in his Silver Ghost cabriolet was like being ferried along the country lanes of Surrey on a small cruise liner.

"Afternoon, Todd," I said to our dashing young chauffeur, who smiled in quite the same knowing manner that my grandfather had just displayed. "What's going on? Why do you both look so…" I searched for the right word. "… smug?"

"I can't imagine what you're referring to, Master Christopher." Todd looked yet more pleased with himself as the tyres spun on the gravel path and he pulled off down the drive.

Grandfather was quick to show his support. "That's right, Todd. Don't tell him what's back at the house yet." His eyes focused on me. "I can see it now. Your mind is running through a thousand ideas, but I'm certain you won't land on the right one."

He was right. Their little secret had plunged me into uncertainty. My grandfather had been promising big things were ahead, and there'd already been talk of sports cars and aeroplanes. His first plan – staging an elaborate ball at his palatial manor at Cranley Hall – had ended in murder and chaos. So it was hard to get too excited about whatever came next.

I simply wasn't the sort of boy to go in for derring-do. I was happier staying at home with a good book (and preferably a slice of cake) than racing about the place looking for dangerous challenges.

"Well, come on then." Grandfather was quite insistent. "You have to guess."

"Oh dear." My head was filled with terrifying challenges. "It's not crocodile wrestling, is it?"

He looked at me like I was missing some brain cells. I was used to such responses from my family and didn't hold it against him.

"Where would I get a crocodile from in Surrey?" His impressive moustaches flattened themselves out in a straight line.

"Knowing you, I'm sure you've got some old friend in The Zoological Society who could open the right doors."

He fell silent for a moment before raising one hand to cover his long white beard. "You've got a point, actually. Not the crocodiles perhaps, but if we were to…" His sentence faded away as he contemplated whatever new spark of an idea I'd put into his head.

I considered having another guess, but he was away with his thoughts. My grandfather did this from time to time. He wasn't your ordinary stuffy old chap. He'd been a famous superintendent for one thing, working for Scotland Yard to bring any number of devious criminals to justice over his forty-year career in the police. He'd only retired when my grandmother had died and he'd… well, he'd shied away from the world. For ten years, he'd featured in my life little more than the stuffed bear in the Cranley Hall entrance parlour. But now, he'd returned to the land of the living to interfere in my very existence.

Fifteen minutes passed without him saying a word. I was sure he'd snap back to life at any moment and, in the meantime, I had the glorious countryside to admire. Is there anywhere more exquisite than England on a sunny day? Can you really find a greater example of the good Lord's eye for detail than when shooting along a light-dappled lane in a Rolls with the drophead down?

On either side of us, there were rolling green fields interspersed with clumps of forest. A prettily bubbling stream ran parallel to the winding road that Todd was steering us along and, up in the sky as Cranley Hall came into view, I caught sight of a Montgolfier-style balloon soaring majestically.

"No!" I instantly exclaimed, causing Lord Edgington to break from his contemplative trance.

"You mean, yes!" He was full of energy once more and leaned forward in his seat to get a better view of the silken orb, which appeared to be hanging in space.

"There's no way I'm going anywhere near that thing. I find cars terrifying enough, and at least they stay on the ground."

Grandfather folded his arms. "Really, Chrissy, I thought we'd moved beyond this. If you don't try new things, you won't know whether you like them."

I doubted his logic. "I've never shot myself in the arm, and I know I don't like that."

"It's no use trying to convince me otherwise. I see your lack of curiosity as a serious problem. If you don't go up in that balloon with me this weekend, you'll regret it for the rest of your life."

"But if I do go up and we come plummeting back down to earth, I'll regret it for the ten seconds that remain of my life before my body is shattered to pieces."

I thought I'd got him then. As we pulled past the gatekeeper's lodge, onto the long drive up to the house, the old boy was speechless. It didn't last long.

He turned to look out of his window and said in a quiet, casual voice. "Your brother's already been for a flight once today." He certainly knew how to get to me; I'll give him that.

"Albert?" I said with more than a hint of disbelief. "My silly, sentimental brother willingly left firm ground to fly with the birds in a giant bag filled with air?"

Grandfather kept his usual calm demeanour. "Not at all. It's filled with hydrogen. Not air."

I didn't reply just then as I was picturing my brother waving down at me from the colourful, floating globe. It was almost impossible to imagine.

"I can't wait," I said without a trace of enthusiasm, but my grandfather didn't notice my sarcasm.

"That's more like it, Chrissy! We'll make a balloonist out of you yet."

CHAPTER TWO

Almost as magnificent as that terrifying contraption in the sky was the sight of Cranley Hall in all its glory. It was an ancient chocolate box sitting prettily amongst the woods, meadows and gardens of the estate. The afternoon sunlight illuminated the pale stone of the building and the historic seat of the marquesses of Edgington looked more regal than ever.

We pulled up at the grand front entrance and the old man threw his door open. "Albert's brought some friends with him, too. They're celebrating the end of their year at university and so I invited them all for the weekend. You'll find them about the house somewhere."

I didn't know how to take this news, but my grandfather's ever-so-friendly golden retriever Delilah was waiting to jump up on me as she did every Friday when I arrived home. My favourite maid, Alice, was there too. Sadly, she didn't jump on me, but delivered a message to Lord Edgington. I might be the tiniest smidgen in love with Alice, and I couldn't help peering at her adoringly as Grandfather ripped open the note and immediately dashed into the house.

"This is fantastic!" He called back over his shoulder and poor old Delilah and I did our best to keep up. "I was worried they wouldn't come in time."

As usual, the famous (and famously single-minded) Lord Edgington didn't wait around to explain what he meant. I had to assume that, having spent the last ten years trapped in an armchair mourning his deceased wife, he had a bank of energy saved up and was determined to use it.

I soon lost sight of the old man as he darted off down a twisting corridor and disappeared into one of the million rooms that my ancestral home contained. I sometimes felt like a zoologist myself in that place. I would occasionally stumble upon a space I'd never spotted before, just as explorers discover new species of birds or butterflies. I'd recently found a room on the lower floor which contained nothing but paintings of cats. Evidently, one of my lofty ancestors had been an admirer of felines. There must have been fifty of the things, all gazing at me through small, dark eyes.

Giving up on finding my grandfather, I heard laughter and walked on down the main corridor of the west wing. I soon came to the billiard room where my brother and his friends were making use of the green baize table.

"Albie, is this your little brother?" a girl with golden-brown hair put her cue down to ask.

I was often shy around new people, but Delilah didn't have that problem and careered into the room with her glossy tail wagging.

"Yes, that's the little monster." I noticed that my brother had put on a more sophisticated voice in front of his four friends. "What do you want, brat?"

I didn't have a chance to answer. That beautiful girl got in first. "Leave him alone, you rotter." She bounded over in my direction, all smiles. "I'm Evangeline and you must be Chrissy. Albert never stops talking about you."

She wrapped me up in an embarrassingly familiar hug, and I'm sure I turned as red as the lampshade over the billiard table.

"You're Evangeline De Vere," I said, as it sank in who this angel sent to earth must be.

My brother looked almost as shy as I was just then. "Evie, we're supposed to be playing a game."

Albert had been in love with Evangeline and spoken of little else for a whole year until she'd cruelly rejected him for…

"Simon Cumberland." A tall, angular sort of chap, who looked a bit like an upturned coat hanger, stuck his large hand out to me from across the room. I felt obliged to go over to him.

"Of course," I said, as the picture I'd had in my head of these people was swiftly replaced by the real thing. "Simon 'Porky' Cumberland! I imagined you being really quite–"

"It's your turn, Simon." Albert held his cue aloft, thus stopping me from pronouncing the word *different*. I can't imagine what he was expecting me to say.

Porky himself didn't look too cheerful either and it suddenly clicked that his unfortunate moniker must have come from his surname being Cumberland, like the sausage, rather than because he was–

"That's Rufus and Hortensia." Albert pointed to the two figures lurking in the background. As I'd already met half the group, I suppose he felt it rude not to introduce me. Hortensia was short with a pointed face, as though someone had recently sharpened her. She wore bright, bold make-up but dark clothes and her lips were the colour of blood. Rufus, on the other hand, had a smiley, approachable demeanour that made me want to have a nice long chat with him about badminton or horses or whatever fun pastimes he might have.

I waved over to them, thrilling in this chance to peek into my brother's life away from our family.

"Why don't you take my place, Christopher?" Hortensia suggested in an appropriately thorny voice. "I'm terribly bored and haven't a clue how to play anyway."

"That's very kind of you, but sport isn't really my thing."

"Oh really?" Evangeline seemed to smile each word out of her lovely mouth and I was quite hypnotised by her. "What is your thing?"

"Chrissy likes cream cakes." Even as my brother uttered the words, I could tell that he regretted them. A smile was just growing on his lips, but it never fully blossomed.

This could have been a genuinely traumatic moment for me; a chubby little chap standing shamefaced in front of my brother's glamourous friends. I might never have lived it down in fact… if Evangeline hadn't been there.

"Oh, me too! I absolutely stuff myself every Saturday morning at my grandmother's house. Can't get enough of the things."

My brother let out an audible sigh of relief and came over to me.

"Chrissy likes birds too." He was clearly trying to make up for his cruelty. "He's awfully knowledgeable about them. If I knew half as much about politics as he does about birds, well, I might even be able to pass my classes back in Oxford."

"Steady on, old man," Rufus joked, and the others laughed warmly.

"Cakes and birds," Evie said, and I adored her a little more – then instantly felt guilty for my true love, Alice, who was probably somewhere polishing something. "You and I have so much in common."

My brother winked at me. "Come along, then, Chrissy. You're on my team."

CHAPTER THREE

At sixteen years old, most boys can only dream of spending time with bright young things such as my big brother's friends. They were all light and cheerful after their balloon ascent, and I had to wonder who was flying the contraption now. After his initial hesitation, my brother warmed to my presence in the group and Evie, as she insisted I call her, treated me more affectionately than she did the dog.

Simon, on the other hand, was a little boring. He didn't stop talking about his new hobby all night.

"I swear parachuting is just like being an eagle. There's no other feeling like it on earth," he told me for the ninth time, as we sat drinking Pimm's cups on the terrace at sunset. "You must try it, Albie. You really must."

"I really mustn't." My brother was not convinced. "Such daredevilry is for soldiers and madmen, and I, my friend, am neither. Going up in the balloon today was thrilling enough."

"I once went flying off my bike when I hit a bump going downhill," cheerful Rufus informed us. "Is it anything like that?"

They all laughed except for Simon, who suddenly grew enraged. "Don't belittle me, Rufus. You're always the first to bang on about whatever new discovery you've come across from ballroom dancing to beetroot. But as soon as I have something to say, you mock and ridicule me."

His girlfriend had managed to keep the smile on her face. "Go easy, darling. He was only pulling your leg."

Simon didn't see it that way. He slammed his fist down on the cast-iron table. "That's easy for you to say. You're never the butt of the joke."

The awkward hush that we'd avoided in the billiard room was now inescapable.

Rufus coughed quietly and tried to make things better. "I didn't mean it like that, old chum. I just…"

Hortensia was staring off across the grounds and spoke as if she hadn't heard a word they were saying. "I always thought beetroot was bad for the stomach. It turns out that it's quite nutritious."

Her change of topic had not gone far enough. Simon's eyes were locked onto Rufus's and would not let go. Up until that point, I'd been happy to imagine that my brother's little clique was the picture of cordiality, but with this odd moment of disproportionate rage, everything changed.

Evie, who had been the very soul of the party until then, seemed to fade before my eyes. Smiley old Rufus became shier and, most surprisingly, Hortensia appeared to be rather enjoying the moment. She lit a cigarette and, between indulgent drags, a smirk formed on her lips as she watched the others' discomfort.

My brother Albert searched for something to distract everyone. "You can't beat a good cocktail, that's what I say!" It did nothing to ease the tension but, luckily at that moment, a new arrival appeared.

"Chet!" They all stood up to welcome an impressive fellow dressed in a knee-length leather pilot's jacket. His hair was as dark as boot polish, and, from his pale eyebrows, I had to conclude he blackened it.

He raced over to us, his strong arms and legs motoring like he was a competitor in an Olympic race walk. I felt rather honoured that he came straight up to me.

"Hey, kid," he said, holding his hand out confidently. "Chet Novicki's the name. Pleased to meet ya."

"Christopher Prentiss." This was as much as I could get out. I was positively bowled over by the charisma the man possessed. He had hair swept back off his forehead in a wave and looked just like one of the American fighter pilots from The Lafayette Flying Corps of the Great War. He might well have been American, in fact, as he had an accent that was impossible to recognise and a surname I couldn't place.

"So you're Albie's baby brother?" He somehow already had a fresh glass of Pimm's in his hand with chunks of cucumber, strawberry and ice in it, though I hadn't seen anyone pour it for him. "Great to have you around, kid. I hear you'll be coming up in the balloon with me tomorrow?"

My words deserted me altogether then. As much as I loved birds, I'd never thought to fly amongst them.

"Chrissy isn't really one for risks and adventures," my brother said, with more generosity than he'd previously spoken of me. "I'm sure he'll enjoy seeing you take off though."

"No, I'll be going." Ahhhh! What was I saying? Me in a balloon

14

filled with hydrogen travelling through the clouds? The very idea of it made me want to run to the woods and live as a wild man. "I can't wait."

Chet's face was reshaped with a winning grin. "That's the spirit, kid. I knew the moment I saw you that I had a flyer on my hands."

Lovely Evie seemed most proud of me then. It was almost enough to make up for the fear that was solidifying within me. My blood had turned to concrete, my guts to stone, as I processed the fact that I had just agreed to go up in Chet's balloon. Perhaps it was his magnetism – or me not wanting to look a coward in front of all those suave individuals – but I had just agreed to go up in his balloon! (I'll say it once more as I was still having trouble coming to terms with this fact.) I, Christopher Aloysius Prentiss, lover of all things pastry based, had just consented to go up (into the sky!) in a contrivance that was lighter than the air around us.

"Does it go very high?" I thought I'd better check before the hole I was digging for myself became so impossibly deep I wouldn't be able to scramble back out of it.

"Well, we ain't going for any record this weekend, but I've got up to ten thousand feet before without too much trouble."

"Ten thousand English feet?" I was hoping that feet where he came from would be a great deal shorter.

"English, Polish, American or Arabian, feet are feet, kid." He smiled at me, then knocked back his drink. "So... what did I miss while I was gone?"

After the bustle and fun of his arrival, this question took us straight back to where we'd been before he came. No one was willing to make eye contact. Even Albert couldn't mumble out a response and we might have stayed that way for some time had our footman Halfpenny not appeared to call us in for dinner.

I fell into step with the – in my mind at least – already legendary Chet Novicki, as we made our way to the dining room. "Isn't it frightening, going up so high like that?"

He looked deadly serious then and stared back off towards the gardens. "There's only one thing that a good balloon pilot is scared of."

I swallowed hard. "What's that?"

"Pointy objects!" He burst into laughter and gave me a resounding thwack to the shoulder. "Come on, kid. I'm starving." He jogged off ahead, and I did not feel any more reassured.

Luckily, Evie was close by and put her arm around me once more. "I wish I had a little brother like you, Chrissy. The only bundles of joy my parents welcomed into our home after I was born were pet geese, and they're hardly the cuddliest creatures."

"A goose once bit my nose," I, for some reason, felt the need to reveal. "My grandmother said it was my own fault for standing too close."

Her soft features were already arranged in a smile, but she managed to look even more enthusiastic. "The exact same thing happened to me, right down to the overbearing grandmother. Old people just don't understand us!"

I felt an awful lot better about my forthcoming death the next day. I'll be honest, I would quite happily have plunged from any great height if it meant I got to see Evangeline De Vere looking so affectionately at me from those heavenly plains. The fact that she was five years older than me, my brother adored her, and she was courting another man didn't enter into my mind for a second. Even though she spoke to me as if I were a pet rabbit or a wounded pigeon, that didn't stop me dreaming that maybe, just maybe, she harboured an intense and spontaneous love for me.

This wasn't the only thing which cheered me up, either. When we took our places at the elaborately laid-out dining table, with its sparkling silver candelabras and shining place settings, the vol-au-vents and appetisers looked delicious. Cranley Hall's cook is known to be, well, eccentric in her choice of ingredients to say the least, but there was nothing out of the ordinary in the fine selection which we all tucked into.

"Best food I've eaten since before the war!" Chet said, and I longed to know more.

"Where did you serve?" my grandfather asked, as he breezed into the room five minutes late.

We stood up out of respect for our host, but he dismissed the gesture with a deferential wave of the hand and sat down in his usual place at the head of the table.

"Royal Flying Corps, Number 54 Squadron. My old man was an engineer at Hendon and I've spent my life tinkering with machines. When the time came, I signed up."

Whenever Chet was speaking, it was as if all the lights in the building had been extinguished. Even my beloved Alice or lovely Evie faded into the background when I was listening to his tales.

"How extraordinary," Grandfather continued. "You must have been little more than a child when the war began."

He smiled at that. "I'm as old as the century is young. They were short of mechanics, so one of the officers helped forge the papers I needed. I was flying missions in a Sopwith Pup by the time I was sixteen. Ground attack mainly, helping our boys on the line."

He was so vivid and youthful that it hadn't occurred to me that Chet was several years older than my brother's group of friends. His confidence and worldliness clearly belonged to a man who had truly lived.

"And now you're at university?" My grandfather was clearly just as enthralled by the chap as I was.

"That's right. I feel like an old fella around these lambs, but I decided I still had more to learn."

"You're not old," Simon said with a laugh in his voice. "You're ancient!" He seemed to have calmed down after his tantrum, and Chet raised his glass in response.

"You know, I've been considering doing something similar myself," Grandfather informed us. "I joined the police when I was fresh from school and didn't think university was for me, but perhaps it's time."

"It's never too late, Lord Edgington," Rufus said with great enthusiasm. "My grandfather's older than you and he swims twice around our lake each morning in nothing but a pair of breeches. It's quite the spectacle."

I was curious about Rufus. He was so friendly and rambunctious but, whenever he spoke, Hortensia was immediately set on edge. Though I assumed, from the familiarity between them, that the two were courting, she could barely stand to return his gaze.

"He sounds like a man after my own heart," Grandfather replied before forcing the conversation around to the topic he really wished to discuss. "Now, which one of you is our parachutist?"

Simon swayed a little in his seat, as though rather proud of himself, which, of course, he was. "That will be me, sir. I'm Simon Cumberland."

Making sure to finish his dainty pastry before responding,

Grandfather clapped his hands together. "Of course! Albert mentioned you some weeks ago, which is why I invited you all today. I have to say, I find the idea remarkable. Throwing yourself from such a height and landing without a scratch on you. Truly remarkable."

It did not take much persuading for Simon to repeat the same lengthy discourse on his favourite pastime that I'd already heard that evening. Even his girlfriend looked bored with hearing quite how many times he'd performed the feat and the rush of energy it inspired. In fact, we were all nodding off when my grandfather surprised us with another revelation.

"Fascinating! And that's why I bought a parachute of my own and will be jumping alongside you tomorrow."

My jaw had fallen open, and my brother looked quite the same across the table. We were like two lazy frogs waiting for flies.

"Surely you're joking, Grandfather?" Albert managed to say before I could. "You can't seriously be considering such an act (at your age)." He didn't actually say these last few words, but the meaning was clear.

"And why on earth shouldn't I?"

Albert looked around at his friends for support. "Well, because you need training. It's not the thing you wake up one morning and decide to indulge in."

"I bought my pack directly from a contact in the American military. It's the latest technology and I've spent the afternoon reading the instruction booklet," Lord Edgington replied, with more than a hint of tetchiness. "I wasn't planning to just try my luck."

"It's really not so complicated," Simon intervened. "I'll be happy to give you a lesson."

"I have no doubt." Hortensia turned away disdainfully. I was coming to wonder if it wasn't just Rufus she was rude to, but anyone who spoke up in front of her.

Having finished our delicious starter, the main meal proved a little more controversial. Though the crème de saumon flans were quite delicious, no one could work out what the oddly rigid chunks inside them were. They tasted like tree bark and looked like metal bolts. Even my grandfather, who was normally our cook's most passionate advocate, couldn't identify what he was eating.

Simon finished talking about parachuting (at last) but his girlfriend found a way to continue the conversation.

"Lord Edgington," Evie began, "may I ask why you decided to try such a dangerous activity?"

Despite having a short temper, and a stare which could melt solid stone, my grandfather had a soft heart and couldn't fail to be charmed by our guest.

"Why, of course." He cleared his throat, like a singer auditioning for a West End revue. "I've made a lot of changes recently. You see, I spent my whole life wondering what sort of person I was supposed to be; decades considering what my parents, my own family and the wider world wanted from me. It was only this year that I came to see that, whatever the answer, it would only set limits upon me."

He paused and looked around the semi-circle of attentive faces. Every last one of us hung on his words. I'd long since realised that, when Lord Edgington spoke, it was best to listen.

"People say that a man of my age shouldn't jump from a balloon or swim in a lake. They'd have you believe that the rich can't befriend the poor, our servants are a different species and men and women will never see alike. And do you know what I say?"

No one dared answer. It was not because we couldn't hazard a guess, but that we knew he'd say it so much better.

"I say, stuff and nonsense." He let out a staccato laugh, and Rufus joined in. "If we spend our lives trying to be a certain kind of person, then we will never learn to be ourselves. That's why I'll be joining Simon and Chet up in that balloon tomorrow and why I fully intend to parachute out of it."

"I like the way you think, sir." Our pilot clicked his fingers down the table. "If there were more people like you, I'd never have had to fly in that damned war in the first place."

The ends of my grandfather's moustaches curled up to point at one another. "Well, I've had a good innings. If the parachute doesn't open and I go hurtling to my death, at least I'll know that I gave it my best shot."

This really pushed the audience into hysterics, and my brother knocked a glass of Bordeaux wine all over his dinner. As the laughter reached new levels of raucousness, I found that I was almost looking forward to the next day's flight.

"I'll be there with you, Grandfather." I actually sounded rather confident for once.

"That's the spirit, Christopher." He smiled straight back at me. "I never doubted you for a second."

CHAPTER FOUR

I'd like to take a moment to explain that I hadn't had a lot of experience drinking alcohol before that day, or chatting away to sophisticated, intelligent women with golden-brown hair. My parents occasionally allowed me a sip of wine, and I was supposed to have a glass of champagne at Grandfather's last birthday (but that went horribly wrong). I was starting to think I should join the temperance movement.

I had half a cup of Pimm's – which my brother insisted was mainly lemonade – and a small glass of red wine and, before I knew it, I'd agreed to leave the earth in surely the most poorly devised form of transportation in human history. I don't think it's exaggerating to say that I would have been happier climbing on the back of an albatross or an extremely large vulture and ascending to the skies. The major advantage of such creatures over hydrogen-filled balloons is that birds are unlikely to be grounded by a small pin!

I woke up the next morning still feeling sore and hazy from the previous night's celebrations. I considered hiding in my room all day to avoid my terrible fate, but grandfather sent someone to fetch me who he knew I couldn't resist. Delilah came wagging her way into my room to place her adorable muzzle on the edge of my bed. She whimpered pleadingly until I roused myself; yet another golden-haired temptress who could bend me to her will.

By the time I had washed and dressed, the others were out on the lawn watching Chet and his two assistants inflate the flying death trap. Up close, the thing was bigger than I'd imagined, but just as beautiful. Beneath a net which secured the internal balloon to the basket, long strips of red, yellow, green and blue silk were attached to a solid metal ring. I think I would have rather enjoyed ballooning if I hadn't had to leave the ground.

Unhappily, Grandfather is very much a man of the morning and always sounds like he's drunk several carafes of coffee by the time I open my eyes.

"Come along, my boy!" Dancing from foot to foot, he was clearly excited about our approaching doom. He was dressed in his traditional grey morning suit and even wore a top hat for some reason.

I took him to one side, as I didn't want the others to think that my liver was in any way lilied. "I don't suppose I could talk you out of-"

He didn't let me finish. "No, but you can watch as Simon over there gives me my parachuting lesson. Who knows, you might like to try it yourself one day."

I considered laughing, or running across the lawn screaming till I could scream no more, but neither quite captured my emotion.

"I think that's unlikely, Grandfather. But I'll lend you my moral support."

"Morning, Chrissy," my brother called. He and his friends were sprawled out on deckchairs as Simon lay out his parachute on the ground. "Have you come for a lesson?"

"In how to be bored to death?" the ever-sarcastic Hortensia added.

"You know what, Horty?" Simon snarled across at her. "That joke is more tiresome than anything I might have to say."

She smiled then, rather innocently. "Oh, I don't know. You haven't started the demonstration yet."

Rufus leaned over to give Hortensia a critical tap on the shoulder. She got the message and stopped her grumbling.

To make up for yet more negativity, Evie shouted a supportive, "Come on, darling. I'm sure you'll be a wonderful teacher." To which Hortensia once more had to turn away in disgust.

Simon set to work describing the different parts of his parachute, and grandfather eagerly engaged in a conversation comparing this simpler design with his innovative new model. There was talk of rip cords and static lines that went way over my head, but I nodded along whenever Simon addressed me and did my best to appear as though I understood what he was saying. He made me try the parachute on to feel the force the wind could enact even down on the ground on a relatively still day.

I have to say that the knowledge of what those two loons were about to do made my ascent in the balloon seem relatively simple. Chet listened to Simon's instructions with a serious expression, and Hortensia couldn't resist the odd snide comment as she sunbathed nearby. The demonstration only made my grandfather more certain of his plan and Evie, Rufus and my brother chatted cheerfully amongst themselves.

When the speech was over, we helped fold Simon's parachute away, and then Halfpenny and Alice served us breakfast on the terrace.

It was the most beautiful morning, and the heat was already rising. A flock of linnets (or possibly just sparrows) were chirping away at one another in the woods, the sky held its pale morning sheen and – with the exception of the honey and mushroom puree, which Grandfather was the only person to enjoy – Cook's breakfast was surprisingly tasty.

When our repast was concluded, Chet got to work consulting his instruments. He occasionally held one finger in the air, to ascertain something no doubt hugely significant that I couldn't quite fathom. We went to the changing rooms on the ground floor, which are normally reserved for tennis in the summer. Simon had a shower and got changed without ever interrupting his complex description of weather conditions, physical forces and timings. The others floated in and out to check he was still boring us and I put on some warmer clothes, as I didn't want to catch a cold up above the clouds.

When we were all ready, we went outside. Grandfather had his neat knapsack parachute on his back and had changed into quite the most informal outfit I'd ever seen him wear. Before that day, I had never imagined that he possessed a pair of slacks. He wore them with braces, a simple white shirt and a red cravat. I have to say he was the picture of a youthful sportsman.

As the three of us walked across the grass to the spot where our aerial chariot awaited, my heart sounded like a woodpecker's beak and my palms were all sweaty. In fact, I was approximately ninety-five per cent sure I was about to die, but still managed to feel rather heroic, despite my brother's heckling.

"Turn back, Chrissy! Turn back before it's too late."

All the staff from the hall had come to witness my final moments, which I thought was jolly nice of them. Alice gave me a little wave, and I instantly felt guilty for ever being in the presence of another woman, let alone one quite so pretty as Evangeline De Vere.

Our chauffeur, Todd, shouted a brief, "Hold on for dear life, Master Christopher," and threw his fist in the air in camaraderie. "I'll pick you up in the van when it's all over."

I assume that Grandfather felt some trepidation himself, as he couldn't leave the earth without a word to the person he admired most in the world.

"Fantastic breakfast this morning, Cook. Really top notch. And what was the extra hint of flavour in the mushroom dish you prepared?"

The brusque, skinny woman had a perpetually chapped complexion, but went a shade redder at the compliment. "That'll be the crushed pilchard, M'Lord."

"Delicious!"

He nodded his thanks, and we took the last few fateful steps towards the balloon. Simon was already aboard and Chet was refilling sandbags for ballast before we disembarked.

"You ready for this, kid?" he asked, as my feet became fixed to the ground and I doubted I would get any further.

"Don't you just know it!" I tried to inject some gusto into my voice, but failed. I sounded like a criminal on the way to the gallows.

"You're going to have the best day of your life." He got that misty look in his eyes once more, which I'd noticed whenever he talked about flying. "I've flown just about every kind of aeronautical known to man, but I wish I could relive my first time."

His preparations complete, he handed any non-essential equipment to his assistants, who were dressed in workman's overalls and would be tasked with collecting the balloon from wherever we landed. We helped my grandfather into the basket and I was happy to see that there really was a bar around the rim for me to hold on to and never let go.

"Good luck, Chrissy," Evie said with a smile, then gave her boyfriend a kiss of which I, Albert and possibly even Rufus looked jealous. There was no sign of Hortensia; she clearly had better things to be doing.

My brother gripped my arm to make sure I couldn't back out, and he and Rufus lifted me inside.

I wasn't the only one who was nervous. Delilah was running around the balloon in a large circle, barking her fluffy head off as Chet's assistants untied us from our moorings.

"No, of course you can't come with us, silly old girl," Grandfather informed his pet, as, apparently, he spoke fluent dog.

The balloon rose a little way into the air and Delilah stopped where she was and made herself as small as possible against the ground. She watched the take-off through woeful eyes. Once a large anchoring weight had been thrown from the basket, we lurched upwards and were soon heading towards the few wispy clouds that were on display that fine day. I'd like to tell you about the way Cranley Hall began to shrink as we ascended, but I'm afraid I was crouched down with my eyes closed, saying a short prayer for my survival.

"This is incredible." Grandfather was experiencing the moment, so that I didn't have to. "Truly the zenith of human achievement."

I cracked my right eye open to see the look of joy on his face, and it was enough to convince me to do the same with the left one.

"That's it, Kid!" Chet encouraged, as he peered at the altimeter and vertimeter which told him our height and rate of climb. His calculations complete, he put his hand down to me and I couldn't resist his winning smile.

Slowly rising from my corner of safety, I peeked over the side of the balloon and it was... "Incredible!"

Seeing the Cranley estate from that height, and the whole ancient Hundred of Edgington around it, was breathtaking. I almost forgot about the fact that there was nothing beneath me for several hundred feet and that one false move could lead to me tumbling from the balloon.

Almost.

"Hello again, Christopher," my grandfather said. To be fair to him, he didn't tell me I was being silly or try to convince me that what we were doing was in any way rational. He simply stood beside me, enjoying the scenery in our tiny box – squashed in together with two other entirely foolish men.

The enormous Cranley Hall lake looked little more than a pond by this point, and the house itself, with its central cube of a building and two extended wings running off it, made me think of a child's toy. It humbled me to see how vast the world was. I could make out Oakton Academy to the west, our village of St Mary-under-Twine nearby and the larger towns of Guildford and Woking to the north and east respectively. In fact, in no time at all, I realised that I could see the whole of London on the horizon, with the dome of Saint Paul's Cathedral clearly visible beneath the exquisite blue sky.

"It's strangely peaceful," I said, once I'd found my voice. My three companions didn't have to say anything to show that they agreed. Like the four points of a compass, we stared out from each corner of the basket at a great swathe of the vista. Facing south, I could see the English coast, beyond the patchwork quilt of fields, hills and hedgerows.

"What did I tell you, Chrissy?" Chet asked as he consulted the readings once more. "And now, Gentlemen, I think it's time to make your exit."

"Fantastic." Simon rubbed his hands together with glee. "The party's about to begin." He got to work, connecting up a strong cord, first to the balloon and then his own parachute. If I'd understood correctly, this was the static line, which would release his chute at just the right moment, once he was clear of the balloon.

Grandfather got busy too, strapping his soft-shell knapsack to his back and ensuring that the belts were securely tightened around his waist and legs.

"You know, I'm rather jealous of you," I told him with a shy smile.

"I was hoping you'd say that, boy, as I bought you a parachute of your own."

I laughed then as I was convinced he was joking. In fact, I even said to him, "You're joking, aren't you?" To which he replied with his usual stony expression and bent down to haul up an extra parachute from the floor.

"I don't joke!" I'm not quite certain that this was true, but he grabbed hold of my shoulder and began his patter. "This is your moment, Chrissy. You didn't want to ascend in this balloon, but you're here now and you've already told me it's incredible. Do you really want to give up the opportunity to fly to the earth like one of your beloved birds?"

There's a word for when you get really nervous and start breathing so heavily that you're not taking in enough oxygen, only I couldn't think what it was just then as it was happening to me.

"I... I've never... never done anything like this before," I said between breaths, but Grandfather had his response already prepared.

"And neither had the many great pioneers who came before you. Think of the very first men and women to jump from such heights. Did they have any experience?"

"No, but I..." Not for the first time, I found myself lost before his superior mind and persuasive stare. I gazed down over the edge of the balloon and it no longer looked so heart-stoppingly terrifying.

"This type of parachute has already saved lives. If I thought there was any great danger involved, I wouldn't be suggesting you join me.

It's your decision, Christopher. It's completely up to you. But, as my grandson, I want you to have all the opportunities that I denied myself for so long because I was simply too frightened to embrace them."

I noticed that our two companions had stopped what they were doing and were eagerly awaiting my response. I glanced down at Cranley Hall one last time. I was too scared to make a sound, but found the courage to nod my head three times and Grandfather clapped his hands together.

"Phenomenal!" He pushed the pack towards me and I turned for him to attach it.

Being able to blame my grandfather for the bad influence he had on me was a rather odd experience. If my father had been there, he'd have been screaming and grabbing hold of me to make sure I didn't do anything so entirely brainless. Of course, my father would never have gone up in a balloon in the first place.

Simon swung his legs out of the basket and sat on the edge. "Good lucky, Chrissy!" With a smile and a wink, he leaned forward and went falling out of sight.

"You've got this, kid," Chet cheered me on, as he pulled on the valve to let some gas from the balloon.

"You remember what to do, don't you, boy?" Grandfather said as he helped me into the same position that Simon had vacated.

"Pull the string and try not to die?" I answered, whilst crossing my fingers that this was a joke.

"Exactly! I checked the pack myself last night, and it's all in working order. You needn't fear any malfunction. You just have to pull the cord to eject the parachute. I'll be right behind you."

I took a deep breath and smiled at my favourite old man. Then, before I could think about it too much and burst into tears, I said goodbye to our pilot and allowed gravity to take me over the edge of the balloon.

Ahhhhhhhhhhhhhhhhhhhhhhhhhhhhhhhhhhhhhhhhhhhhhhhhhhhhhhhh! I think this just about sums up how I felt for the next few seconds. Just to confirm it, I believe I emitted the noise, "Aiiiiiiiiiiiiiiiiii iiiiiiiiiiiiiiiiiiiiiiiiiiiiiiiiiiiiiiiiiiiiiiiiiiiiiiiii!" as I shot through space towards the green and pleasant hills of Surrey.

It suddenly occurred to me that the very real, physical terror I was feeling might prevent me from activating the muscles in my arms, or that the force of the air that was bombarding me would stop me reaching the small metal ring I needed to access. Luckily, those ideas were soon disproved.

I pulled the cord, my parachute opened, and I was immediately yanked up into the air by the strength of the silken life-protector as it inflated. And then… peace. I had thought so much about the short period when my body would be in freefall that I hadn't considered what came after it. There was a serenity to my descent that I could never have foreseen. I was a leaf caught by the breeze, an osprey gliding on a thermal wind. Despite the force of air that was pounding against my chute, it was surprisingly quiet up there. I half wished I had a book to read.

Instead, I looked around at the glorious scenery. There was my sprawling ancestral home, half in shadow, half light. I could make out the South Downs in all their hilly splendour and even spotted the Hurt Wood windmill, with its wooden sails turning. Descending through the skies, it was easy to believe that we'd never left the Garden of Eden. The world beneath me was so great and so green that it was hard to imagine any parallel.

I hadn't paid enough attention when Simon had been telling us how to steer, but tried to pull on the straps as best I could to stay within the Cranley estate and land in the meadow that Simon and my grandfather had agreed would be their target. All my fear came speeding back to me when the time came to land. I pictured myself breaking my ankles or crashing into a cow, but, in the end, it was quite uneventful. I pointed my toes down, kept my eyes at a forty-five-degree angle to the ground, and even managed to land in a roll to dissipate the momentum.

Standing back up again was the hardest part. I was planning to jump to my feet and whoop out an exultant celebration, but the wind was too strong and the parachute tugged me towards the woods. It took me a minute to get the damned thing under control, by which time my grandfather had landed nearby with all the grace I'd expect from him. To my surprise, he looked alarmed as he detached his own parachute with ease.

"I don't know how it could have happened," he said, and I was more than a little confused. "His line was fixed correctly. The chute should have opened!"

He went running past me through the long grass, so I unclipped my knapsack, stepped out of the leg straps and followed him. Moments later, we came to a muddy patch of ground at the side of the meadow where Simon was lying face down.

"No one could survive a fall like that." Despite this statement, Grandfather knelt down beside the body to check for a pulse. "The poor chap's dead."

CHAPTER FIVE

It wasn't fear that gripped me then, but anguish and disgust. I'd been so distracted by my own bravery, and all the pretty scenery, I'd failed to notice that Simon's parachute had never opened. He'd dropped like a lead weight to the ground.

As my grandfather turned the body over, I-

I'm sorry. I just remembered the sight of poor, dead Simon and changed my mind about finishing that sentence. It was enough to put me off pudding for a week! The bloody image will never leave me, but Grandfather's old police instincts kicked in and he examined the man's injuries, then looked for a fault in the parachute.

"The line was cut," he diagnosed, as I came to stand next to him. He pointed to a folded white cord on the back of the pack. "This length of rope was supposed to unfurl and trigger the launch of his chute. Half of it came out before it reached the break, but then... nothing."

"Couldn't it just be an accident?" I asked, wishing it were true.

My grandfather didn't respond immediately, but continued poking at the knapsack with a gloved finger. "Very unlikely. The cut here, the frayed ends – they're too clean to have worn down over time and it's not as though there was anything to rub on that part of the cord. I can only conclude that someone tampered with the parachute before we went up into the air."

"So it's murder?" I said,

The shock finally hit me. We'd worked our way through one arduous investigation a few weeks earlier and here we were again, on the hunt for a killer.

Grandfather didn't answer. He was hard at work. "Did you notice the black marks all over the parachute?"

I leaned in closer to see what he was talking about and spotted the greasy smears. "It looks like shoe polish."

"Or perhaps engine oil." He put one finger against the largest stain. "No, you're right, it's not greasy enough to be oil."

Just then, we heard a car rumbling along the lane beside the meadow and Todd pulled to a halt. "We saw something fall from the balloon," he shouted over as he jumped from the Morris van which the gardeners normally used to carry equipment. "Miss Evangeline is going out of her mind with worry. She says that she never saw Simon's parachute."

In the calm, emotionless voice he always used to break bad news, my grandfather said, "Yes, I'm afraid it failed to open. Simon's dead." He glanced once more at the victim, then nodded to himself as if to confirm what he'd been thinking. "You'll need to stay here, Todd. You can flag down the police when they arrive. I'll return to the house with Christopher. I'd like to talk to any witnesses before the police get in my way."

"Very good, M'Lord." Todd bowed his head and stepped aside to leave the path to the van clear.

As we walked over to the vehicle, I could see that former Superintendent Edgington was away with his thoughts. He barely looked at me as he waved an absentminded hand through the air.

"Chrissy, you'll drive, won't you? I really need to think this over."

Now it was my turn to deliver some bad news. "I don't know how. And, before you suggest otherwise, this is not the moment to learn."

He nodded resignedly and opened the driver's door to the racing-green van. Luckily for me, it did not have the acceleration of an Alfa Romeo or the top speed of an Aston Martin. Of course, this didn't stop Grandfather from shooting us along the bumpy lane with the pedal to the floor. It was more frightening than our aerial activities by a substantial factor.

When we stepped out of the vehicle at the side of the house, Evie spotted us and fell to her knees on the lawn. I thought that the boys would have been only too happy to comfort her, but it fell to Hortensia in the end. The two girls embraced, which, now that I thought about it, was surely the first direct communication I'd seen between them all weekend.

"You'll have worked it out, of course, but I'm afraid to tell you that Simon's parachute did not open and he was killed in the fall." Grandfather paused to look around the usually bright faces of my brother and his friends. "I'll need to speak to each of you in turn, but, for the moment, you should stay here together. Rufus, there's a telephone in the petit salon. Please call the police. Albert, you'll be coming with me to the changing rooms."

He didn't wait for a reply, but marched off past them for my brother and me to catch up. I'd already caught glimpses of what our grandfather was capable of as an investigator, and I found the cold determination that ran through him at such moments impressive. Policing was still a part of him and, even though he'd been retired for over a decade, it was a mantle he could pull back on with ease.

He led us past the terrace steps and round through an inconspicuous white door, which gave onto a number of small offices, storage rooms and the changing area where we'd all been that morning.

Before we went any further, I needed to get something straight in my mind. "You think that someone cut the line when the parachute was in here, don't you? But surely anyone could have tampered with it at any given time."

Grandfather came to a stop in the middle of the communal area and peered around the room. To our left were several cabins, each with doors painted in a different bright colour. A slat bench ran along one wall, and there were showers and other facilities in the adjoining bathroom. With his scan complete, he deemed to answer my question.

"You're wrong there. Simon opened his parachute when he was instructing us this morning. The only time it could have been interfered with was between then and the time he got into the balloon. Which means the only possible killers are Albert and his friends."

"Excuse me, I didn't kill anyone." My brother's voice had the tendency to rise sharply whenever he was distressed, and he sounded like a parrot just then.

Grandfather tutted. "I'm not suggesting for a second that you are."

The old man's words clearly weren't reassuring enough, as Albert still wasn't happy. "But…?"

There was no immediate response. Instead, Grandfather walked over to the spot where he'd left his clothes and pulled his long grey coat down to cover his more casual attire. He swished it through the air and it parachuted out for him to slot his arms through one by one. As it settled over his figure, I could tell just what it meant for him to be suitably attired. His morning dress was a uniform, and he was himself once more.

He turned to address my brother. "You must admit, my boy, you had a very good reason to kill the man."

Albert's eyes grew wide with outrage. "Simon and I have known each other since our first day at university."

"That may well be, but you've spent the last month brooding because you were in love with his girlfriend and she rejected you to be with him. The police will want to know all about it."

"I… He…" My brother had run out of verbs.

"Do you think that Evie could have something to do with this?" The note of fear in my voice forced my grandfather to look at me with just as much suspicion as he'd previously viewed Albert.

"It hasn't escaped my notice that Evangeline De Vere is a very attractive woman. You should never underestimate the power that beauty has in this world. Whether it be that of another person, a rare gem, or a great work of art. In my experience, it's often enough to make a man kill."

The three of us fell quiet as we considered the implications of Grandfather's words. In the end, he was the one to break the silence.

"I need to get the time clear in my mind, but there was a period when Chrissy and I were getting changed and Simon was in the shower. I heard the others milling about in here, which is when I believe that one of you took the opportunity to cut the line." He followed the bench to the corner where Simon's clothes were hanging. His eyes flicked from object to object without touching anything. "Albert, do you remember a particular moment when one of your friends was in here alone?"

My brother was clearly still struggling with the morbid development and went to sit in a chair at the side of the room. "I really don't know. As you said, we were going back and forth. I saw that Chet stopped by at one point to tell you that he was ready to launch. Hortensia couldn't resist peeking in to tease Simon – or at least that's what she told us she was doing. And Rufus came to make use of the facilities, whilst Evie and I were having some tea."

Grandfather stopped what he was doing to cast his gaze across my brother's hesitant face. "So you're saying Evangeline never entered this room on her own. Are you sure of that?"

He hesitated, and we all knew the answer. "Sadly, no. She came back here after we'd left because she wanted Simon to wear her scarf when he jumped. She said he'd done it each time, and it had brought him good luck."

"Which has evidently just run out." Grandfather peered down at the small pile of Simon's possessions and, with a despondent sigh, reflected on a life cut short. "It's a tragedy by anyone's standards that a boy with so much of his life to enjoy could be erased from our world with one snip of scissors or slash of a knife. Well, I promise you this..."

He never made that promise, as he had something more useful to offer. Crouching down low, he carefully moved aside a light summer jersey and, between the tips of his gloved fingers, picked up a single strand of hair.

"Golden brown," I muttered in a half whisper, but Grandfather hadn't finished.

Placing the discovery into a tiny envelope, which he apparently carried for just such an occasion, he moved on. He went through each item of clothing but left the scene exactly as we'd encountered it. Just when it seemed that there was nothing left to find, he placed his fingers in the gap between two slats in the long wooden bench and chanced upon a small, folded pocket knife.

I read off the inscription on the handle. "R. L. S."

"Rufus Longfellow-Slaughter," my brother revealed. "That little blighter."

CHAPTER SIX

A force of energy once more, Grandfather was up on his feet.

"As I've told your brother on any number of occasions, Albert, we must never jump to conclusions." He was out of the door before we knew what to think.

With the pace of a much younger man, he strode back outside and pointed to Rufus. "You, upstairs, this moment."

The young man was sitting on a bench with Hortensia draped all over him. Her head was resting on his shoulder and she looked very comfortable there indeed. He almost jumped out of his skin at the words, and instantly leapt up to standing to cover his shock. Hortensia was left to sprawl out on the bench rather awkwardly.

Not another sound was made as we left the two girls alone and Rufus trailed after us up the elaborate stone staircase. The petit salon is not the grandest room in Cranley Hall, but it has a rather homely charm. In addition to the golden chandeliers and gilt panelling that you would expect from a luxurious space in one of the richest houses in England, there is a thick and cosy Chinese carpet and photographs of different members of my extended family displayed on a wall beside the door.

Cosy, however, was not the atmosphere my grandfather required in order to interrogate our first suspect. He pulled a high-backed chair out from a corner table and placed it against a bare wall, then signalled to Rufus to sit down. Not only would there be no comfy sofa for him, he'd have to sit there stewing as the three of us huddled in the far corner to confer.

"Albert, what can you tell me about your friend?" Grandfather asked in a whisper.

I saw my brother revert to his usual, happy-go-lucky self. "He's an awfully nice chap. I can't imagine he'd hurt a fly."

Grandfather wasn't impressed. "You know, I doubt such an argument would stand up in court!"

Albert swallowed, as he realised what the great detective was implying. "Oh, I see. Well, you might have a point." He paused for a moment to think of something more helpful. "His father is Matthias Longfellow-Slaughter, the newspaper mogul. Quite the man about town, by all accounts. He and Rufus do not see eye to eye."

"What about his relationship with your friends, though?" He peered over his shoulder at our suspect. "There was something oddly hollow about him at dinner last night that I couldn't quite define."

"Well, yes," my brother said. "He can be rather dozy at times, but he's a bang-up chap."

"Fine." Grandfather waved the point away with an impatient hand. "What else can you tell me about him?"

My brother scratched his cheek before replying. "Well, Ru's a dab hand at badminton, he mixes a rather tasty brandy Alexander, and he and Hortensia have had a thing together ever since we were freshers."

"A thing?" My grandfather could never abide slang and seemed quite lost by Albert's babbling.

"Yes, you know. A relationship. But it's on one moment, off the next. Only they can tell you for certain what's going on between them."

"Simon didn't seem to like him." They turned to me in surprise, as they'd clearly forgotten I was there. "Out on the terrace last night, when you were plying me with liquor, Simon took offence at something that Rufus said."

For once, Albert seemed a little introspective. "That was just two boys ragging one another. We were all best of friends. I solemnly swear." He sounded far less confident than he had a few minutes earlier.

Presumably thinking that he could get little else out of his light-hearted grandson, Lord Edgington spun on his heel and walked over to start the interview. He had just opened his mouth when Rufus interrupted.

"Please tell me it's not her. I couldn't live thinking that she'd done something to hurt Simon."

"What makes you think that anyone hurt Simon?" Grandfather was quick to respond.

Rufus's eyes flicked between Albert and me at the back of the room. "I'm sorry. I just assumed that you had me call the police because his death was suspicious. And... well, it's no secret that Hortensia and Simon didn't get along. So, I..."

Grandfather raised his chin and looked at Rufus through narrow slits. I couldn't actually see his face, but that was what he did whenever a witness made an unexpected point.

He took a few steps back and forth in front of us before continuing.

"So you think that Hortensia would have killed your friend Simon out of...?"

"Jealousy perhaps?" Rufus didn't sound too sure himself. "As much as Hortensia and Evie have been best friends since they were children, it's not always clear whether they actually like one another. Dear Horty always wants whatever Evangeline has."

"So Hortensia was in love with Simon. Is that what you're saying?" Grandfather paused to peer over his shoulder for Albert's take on the situation. Sadly, my big brother was already quite flummoxed by the unfolding story.

"I think love is a bit of a strong word. After all, Horty and I are really very fond of one another. I just think that she can be a little envious of people who have more than her."

Grandfather pulled up a chair of his own. "'Really very fond of one another'? And if we ask Hortensia about your relationship, what will she say?"

There was no fear in Rufus's voice as he replied. "Oh, I imagine she'd agree. I admit there was a time when I thought she might love me, but she's always told me that she didn't want to be tied down."

"So you love her then?" Grandfather asked with surprise in his voice. "You were the one who wanted more and would have done anything for her?"

"Yes, I suppose that's true." His words got stuck for the briefest of moments before firing out of him. "Yes, I love her. I don't think there's anything wrong with that."

"Jolly good, Ru-Ru!" my brother cheered, and I could tell that our grandfather wished he'd asked him to wait outside.

"You'd have done anything for her," Grandfather repeated. "Even murdering her rival's suitor to satiate her long-standing jealousy?"

Rufus frowned like he was having a thoroughly hard time understanding the purpose of such a question. "Now, steady on. I wouldn't have killed Simon. He was a wonderful chap. I'm absolutely heartbroken over what happened. We all are."

Grandfather nodded and turned his head at a sympathetic angle, as if to apologise. I knew it was an act. I'd seen him interview suspects before, and this was just a prelude to the main event. He was waiting for the perfect moment to reveal what he knew.

"Yes, it's terribly sad," the old man said without feeling, and then reached into the fob pocket of his long coat. "I don't suppose you'd care to inform us how your knife ended up among Simon's possessions, just beneath the spot where his parachute was hanging?"

Rufus was flabbergasted. He stared at the small mahogany-handled knife and the three silver letters glinted in the daylight, which streamed in through the high windows.

"I…" this was as far as he got, but I could see that he was piecing a case together of his own. "My mother gave me that knife on my eighteenth birthday. I had it in my room upstairs, anyone could have taken it."

"Or you could have cut the line and dropped the knife when someone happened upon you there." Grandfather's voice seemed to take on an almost demonic edge whenever he laid out his accusations. It had a depth and resonance that I'd never heard from another person.

"So then why wouldn't I have gone back for it after you went up in the balloon?" Rufus was starting to sound really very irked.

Grandfather sucked in air between his teeth. "Well, yes. That's a very good point, Rufus. You'd make a fine policeman." This seemed to appease Albert's previously cheerful friend, but Grandfather had a new line of enquiry to explore. "You seemed quite sure that Hortensia was capable of murder when we came in here. A petty jealousy between friends is hardly reason to think she could be violent. Is there something else you'd like to tell me?"

There was a conflict running through Rufus. He'd argued himself into a corner and was clearly caught between telling the truth and painting his girlfriend as a killer.

"No, it's not that. I assumed you wanted to talk to me first because of her, that's all. And I only thought of Hortensia because I couldn't see who else would have had the faintest interest in hurting Simon."

"What about Albert?" Grandfather didn't look around to see my brother's face collapse.

"Albert?" Understandably, Rufus was surprised to hear Lord Edgington implicate his own grandson.

"Grandfather!" Understandably, my brother wasn't too thrilled either.

"Yes, Albert Prentiss," the wily old chap continued. "He's standing just behind me. You know the fellow; floppy fringe, puppy dog eyes, normally heartbroken over some girl or other. And, as it happens, he's spent the weeks since your university dance crying those puppy dog eyes out over one Evangeline De Vere. The girlfriend of the man who was just murdered."

Rufus had to concede defeat. "Well, yes, I suppose you're right. Albert did have a pretty good motive."

"Rufus!" As parrots go, my brother possessed a stunningly good vocabulary. He came marching forward to force his way into the conversation. "You know I'm not the sort to murder a chap over a lovely girl. Yes, I admit that I went a little off the deep end when Evie chose Simon over me, but he was my chum."

Grandfather turned to look up at him. "You're not the sort to murder someone, but you've said the same thing about our every last suspect. We know when the parachute was sabotaged, and we know who had access to the changing room, so who could the killer be?" He glanced between Albert and Rufus. "Christopher and I hadn't met your friends until yesterday, which only leaves Evie, Hortensia, the two of you and-"

"Chet!" Albert and Rufus exclaimed at the same moment, and they both looked very pleased with themselves.

CHAPTER SEVEN

"Do you really think Chet could be the killer, Grandfather?"

The boys had left us and the old detective had relocated to an armchair to have a good think until our pilot returned in the retrieval lorry.

"I don't know yet." After all the energy he'd expended in the first hour of our investigation, he now seemed a little deflated. "It's a puzzle, it really is. As far as we know, none of the friends would gain financially from Simon's death. Beyond jealousy, lust or a joke that's gone wrong, I can't think what would have driven one of them to do such a thing."

I could tell that he needed someone to help him along for once, but my ideas normally proved to be so far from the mark that they weren't worth uttering in the first place. "If Chet was involved, perhaps he's not who he says he is."

"Oh, really?" He at least sounded interested in my idea.

"And perhaps Simon found out the truth and so Chet cut his parachute to keep him quiet."

"Quite preposterous!" He sounded less interested.

"No, wait, listen," I said, to slow things down. "Chet's rather impressive, don't you think? But there's something unusual about him. Did you notice that he talks a lot without giving much away? In all the time we've spoken, I never once heard him mention the names of any of his friends or even his family."

Grandfather looked up at me, his brow now furrowed. "How interesting."

Chet was already something of a hero to me, and I didn't want to think badly of him. But if we could rule out the other boys, and perhaps even Hortensia, surely, he was a likely suspect.

"He said that his father was a mechanic, but the story of how he made it into the flying corps at such a young age didn't ring true somehow."

"Is that right, kid?" came a voice from the open door. "And why do you say that?"

I looked up to see Chet's dark, handsome face peering back at me. My whole body cringed.

"Oh, gosh. I'm so sorry, Chet. I wasn't saying that you were lying exactly. I just meant that-"

He took a few steps into the room and pulled his heavy leather coat off. "Relax, kid, I'm messing with you. As it happens, I *was* lying. I do that a lot."

Grandfather had been watching this interchange with quiet interest and decided to make his presence known. "I'm tired of being in here. I think we should take a stroll." He stood up, and, instead of leading us back outside as I'd been expecting, turned towards the internal corridor.

"You mentioned yesterday that you like art, Chet. I thought I might show you the gallery in the east wing." He didn't wait for an answer but shot off along the hall, heading to the oldest part of the house from where we could access Cranley's substantial art collection.

"It was my great-great-grandfather, I believe, who started buying up half the artworks in Europe, as a man today might collect cigarette cards." He spoke like a guide at a museum. He did not look around to check whether Chet and I were following as he streamed through the cavernous entrance hall. "I think you'll be rather impressed."

Cranley is a gigantic old place, and we conducted the rest of our three-minute journey with nothing but the beating of our feet on the Spanish Azulejo tiles for accompaniment. When we reached the eastern gallery, Grandfather struggled with the door. I doubt anyone had been there in years and it seemed to have glued itself shut.

Forcing his way inside, he turned back to the offending portal and put his arms out rather grandly. "Welcome."

I couldn't glean what he was trying to do by taking us there. Back in the petit salon, it seemed as though Chet was about to confess to something when Grandfather had interrupted. Just weeks before, I would have dismissed this as the foibles of an old man, but I knew now that everything Lord Edgington did had a clearly defined purpose behind it. He was a master manipulator and a man of singular intuition.

Perhaps he'd wanted Chet to be nervous, leaving him to question what we already knew about him and think up hasty explanations for his actions. Or perhaps my grandfather really was tired of being in that part of the house. When a man has over a hundred rooms, why not make the most of them?

"Is that a Titian?" Chet ran past us to examine a renaissance portrait of the Holy Family. Even I was impressed by the richness of the blues and golds that leapt out of the frame. It looked like it had only just been painted.

"It is." Grandfather smiled to see the man's excitement. "I used to come down here all the time when I was younger. It's been shut up for too long."

In the centre of the room, there were a number of chairs covered over with heavy burgundy blankets. Like a weary bullfighter, Lord Edgington pulled one of the coverings to the floor and a cloud of dust took to the air.

"Won't you have a seat?"

Chet accepted the offer, and my grandfather prepared a chair of his own, just opposite. At times like this, it was difficult to know exactly why the old man kept me around. Perhaps my inferior take on his cases helped put his own far sharper views into perspective. Right then, I didn't even know where to stand, so I hovered where I was in the space behind our suspect.

Neither man said anything at first, but the pilot's eyes had fallen on a rather gloomy painting of a cleric in long black robes. "Tell me that's not a Caravaggio," he uttered, with some disbelief.

Grandfather half turned around, as though he hadn't planned to end up in that exact spot for Chet to notice that exact painting. "I'm afraid I can't, as it wouldn't be true."

"Wow!" Chet shook his head as he processed the list of masterworks that he was surrounded by. "What did your great-great-granddaddy do to stump up the cash for a Titian and a Caravaggio?"

I could see that the real interrogation was about to begin. Grandfather's face had become fixed, his elaborate moustaches were arranged in one long, unyielding line, and he turned back to glare at his prey.

"Caravaggio was a murderer, you know? An absolute genius with the brush, of course, but a thug nonetheless. Did you kill Simon?" He delivered the accusation almost nonchalantly, as though it were really only an afterthought.

Chet just smiled. "I'm not much of a painter and I'm no murderer either."

"But you are a liar." This wasn't a question. Former-Superintendent Edgington was stating facts. "Or at least, that's how you described yourself."

For the first time since I'd met him, Chet appeared less than infinitely confident. "It's true, but I have my reasons."

"And they are?"

The balloonist leaned forward in the chair and placed his hands together in front of him. "I've only changed who I am because I couldn't be the person I really was." He brought his fine eyebrows together and seemed aware of just how opaque his sentence was. "I trust that whatever I have to tell you won't go any further than this room?"

Grandfather crossed one leg over the other and nodded silently.

"Well then, I don't mind telling you that Novicki is my mother's name."

"You never knew your father?" the interviewer asked with a hint of tenderness.

"Oh, I knew him alright, though I sometimes wish I hadn't. You see, my mother came over from Poland after the Pogrom of 'eighty-one."

"She was Jewish?"

"That's right and things weren't great for her people in those days. In fact, they're probably not a great deal better today. Anyway, Matka came from a wealthy family, but my grandparents didn't like the way the wind was blowing, so they sent her to Britain. The money they gave her didn't go too far over here, but my mother was smart. She spoke three languages and took a job as a governess in a grand house in the south of England. The Duke of Luton's house, to be precise, and the Duke of Luton is my father."

I let out a noisy breath. The reason why Chet had constructed such a diaphanous identity for himself was beginning to make sense. Grandfather looked up at me knowingly before continuing with his next question.

"So you weren't acknowledged by your father. Is that what you're saying? You had to pretend to be someone you were not."

Chet let out a full laugh right then and needed a moment to recover. "Sorry, but you couldn't be further from the truth. My father is shameless and paraded me in front of his family as a badge of pride. I was his beautiful baseborn boy, his *nullius filius*. He wallowed in the shock and horror I would cause his poor wife and daughters. He even kept my mother as his mistress in an apartment in their house. He's a cruel and twisted man, who knows how to be generous when it suits him."

Chet's tone had darkened, and he stared at a scene of a beheaded martyr beside the Caravaggio as he unfurled his tale. "What I told you about my father being a mechanic is true. He was forever tinkering about with cars, planes and various useless inventions when I was a kid. He had no other sons, so he liked to have me there to tell him how wonderful he was. I enjoyed it and, when the time came, he was the one who got me a job at the aerodrome and convinced a squadron leader he knew in the flying corps to overlook my tender age."

Grandfather studied the man for a moment. "And nobody there knew who you really were?"

"Nobody there or at Oxford or anywhere else since I left home. And I like it that way. I was born in Britain to a British father, but everywhere I go people treat me as an exotic outsider; some sort of pet half-breed. Though that might not suit everyone, it works for me."

I noticed that, as he was speaking, his voice had become posher and more English.

"What about your accent then? Have you never been to America?" I felt sure he must have an American connection in there somewhere.

"No, kid." He put the voice back on for me. "But Chet Novicki can be anyone he wants."

"Could you be a killer?" Grandfather asked, forcing another stab of laughter from Chet.

"I already am one." He left the words to settle for a moment, and my heart beat a little faster until he explained. "I shot down a German Halberstadt on one of my first raids. I wouldn't be surprised if the pilot died before the plane hit the ground. I killed for my country, but I had nothing to do with Simon's chute not opening."

"So, as an expert yourself on all things aeronautical, can you explain what happened?" Grandfather kept veering between sympathetic and confrontational to keep our witness off guard. I could see that the tactic was working; despite his surface confidence, Chet couldn't get a grip on the conversation and struggled to defend himself.

"I'd have to think that the static line on the parachute broke somehow."

"It was cut."

"All right, someone cut it. But it wasn't me."

Grandfather nodded as though accepting the claim at face value. "You must admit, it would require some knowledge of the technical aspects of Simon's parachute to know the best way to sabotage it."

"I do. But you must admit that Simon had talked about nothing else since we got here yesterday and even his doting girlfriend looked bored out of her pretty skull to have to hear about it for another second."

"Touché!" The old man seemed happy to have such a worthy opponent before him. "What of Evangeline herself and these youngsters you've been spending your time with? How exactly did you come to be friends?"

"She picked me up in a bar, if you must know." Chet had the ability to make quite the most shocking revelations sound innocent. "She said she found me fascinating and we should spend more time together."

"So you were attracted to her?"

He didn't need to think long to answer. "Have you seen the girl? She's like the Venus de Milo made flesh. Of course I was attracted to her. But then I met Simon, and we became good friends. I could tell they were head over heels for one another and realised I never stood a chance. You see, Simon had a daddy that he could talk about in public and I have war stories and a mysterious background."

"Ah, I see." I'm certain that Grandfather adopted an elderly tone to his voice in order to lull his victims – sorry, suspects – into a false sense of security. "Yes, that's very nicely put. And I assume your eagerness to distance yourself from your father would explain why you use blacking to darken your hair?"

Chet turned his head to the side, presumably trying to work out where my grandfather was taking us with this new train of thought. "Well, no, actually. I just think it makes me look kind of handsome."

"But it does explain why there were black marks all over Simon's parachute?"

A hostile silence fell between the two men. Standing just a few feet away, I could almost feel the air grow colder.

Chet straightened his back and stuck his chin out defiantly. "I don't know anything about that. I must have told you five times already that

I had nothing to do with his death and I'm mourning the kid just like everyone else."

In one abrupt motion, Grandfather rose to standing. "Yes, just like everyone else. You're all so terribly sorry that the poor boy fell several thousand feet to his death and not one of you could have crept into the changing room this morning to cut his line with the pocket knife I discovered there. The pocket knife which, oh so helpfully, points to Rufus as the killer."

Chet had no response to that but to slump deeper into the armchair, his words and breath apparently exhausted as my grandfather swept from the room.

CHAPTER EIGHT

"There's no time, boy," Lord Edgington told me as we thundered back through the house. "The police will be here any minute and we'll lose the opportunity to find out what really happened."

I don't exactly have a runner's physique and was winded from trying to keep up with him. "But where are we going? You just made it sound as though Chet was the killer."

He glanced at me through the side of his vision. "Really, Christopher, I thought you'd know better than that by now. I have no concrete reason to believe Chet would have killed Simon. I was merely drumming some fear into him to see what he'll do. All we ended up with was a pretty story and a determination on my part never to cross paths with the Duke of Luton."

"But the black marks all over the parachute? That was so clever of you to identify them. Surely that puts Chet in the frame?"

"It does nothing of the sort. If we take it as given that Rufus's knife was planted at the scene, it only makes sense that the killer would have done the same thing with the black hair colouring on the parachute and the smudge of red lipstick on the collar of Simon's shirt. Someone is trying to throw us off the scent, but it's still not apparent who that might be."

I didn't like to tell him that I hadn't spotted any red lipstick when we'd examined Simon's clothes, though that clearly hinted to Hortensia having a hand in the crime. Evie was far more natural and barely wore a trace of makeup. It made me curious that he hadn't mentioned the final piece of physical evidence we'd discovered. "And what about the hair we found? Don't you think that the killer planted it?"

He stopped in the entrance hall and glanced around at the faces of all those horrid taxidermic animals. "It's hard to say." He approached the mount of a rather vicious boar and looked the creature right in its glass eyes. "Lipstick, the pocket knife and hair blacking jump out at you, but a single hair could easily be overlooked. I'm not certain that it was planted."

This hit me much harder than I might have expected. My hands were shaking as he stopped trying to scare the dead pig and accelerated off once more. It wasn't just the thought of Evie being involved in her boyfriend's murder that had got to me, but what that might imply.

"Grandfather," I struggled to get the words out. "Have you really ruled out Albert?"

"No, of course I haven't." He spoke with all his usual resolve. "He had a perfectly good motive and just as much opportunity as anyone else to carry out the crime."

"It's just-"

He didn't let me finish. "It's just that, if Evie and Albert were the only ones the killer didn't leave any evidence to implicate, you're worried that your brother was involved."

He'd read my mind. It wasn't the first time he'd performed such a trick. I could never hide my feelings from him, and I have to say I found it quite unnerving.

"That's right."

"Well, I'm glad you finally got there, Chrissy, but I wouldn't worry too much. Your brother is quite the softest, soppiest human on earth and would just as likely climb into a boxing ring or conquer Mount Everest as murder one of his friends."

He'd made me feel a touch better by saying this, but I still had more questions for him.

"So who do we talk to next?"

"I think that the time has come to have a conversation with the woman who glues this whole group together."

"Evie?" This seemed like the only possible answer but, as this was Grandfather I was talking to, I was inevitably wrong.

"No, of course not. She can wait. It's Hortensia who interests me."

I spent the next few minutes, as we tracked down our suspect, trying to work out the logic of anything he'd just said. I did not succeed.

Hortensia and Rufus had their arms around one another on a picnic blanket on the great lawn. She appeared to have spent the morning crying and he couldn't help looking pleased to be so close to the woman he loved. It was rather sweet that something good could blossom from something so tragic. I just hoped Haughty Hortensia wouldn't jilt the poor fellow as soon as her tears had dried.

"May I have a moment?" Grandfather enquired in an exceedingly polite manner. I wasn't used to hearing him speak so softly.

She glanced at her beau, who nodded his head supportively and helped her to her feet. As she did so, the first police car pulled along the drive, but it was just the local bobbies. Grandfather wouldn't be too worried about such inexperienced officers getting in his way. It was his old rival Inspector Blunt of Scotland Yard he was looking out for. I had no doubt that the odious man would put an end to our investigation the moment he set foot on the Cranley estate.

Grandfather issued another order before our interview could begin. "Rufus, you'd better deal with the police. You can tell them whatever they want to know, just keep them away from me."

"Yes, sir," the boy replied and, with a gentle kiss for his girlfriend, he hurried off towards the house.

"I'm glad you have someone to support you through this difficult time," Grandfather told the young lady, who had got changed since I'd been with her that morning and wore a striking red and black dress to match her bright lips and shaded eyes.

She cast her gaze back across the grass. "Yes, he's been really very sweet." Her usual note of boredom was present in her voice. Perhaps "sweet" wasn't what she was looking for in a man.

Grandfather motioned for her to sit back down on the blanket and pulled up a deckchair of his own. As usual, I wasn't sure where I was supposed to fit in, so I plopped myself down on the grass. I couldn't imagine anyone objecting to that.

"I heard that you and Evangeline grew up as friends." I noticed that Grandfather had positioned himself so that Hortensia was forced to look into the sun. That crafty old duck.

There was a selection of nibbles laid out across the blanket, from scotch eggs to pork pies, but Hortensia seemed happy to eat them with her eyes alone.

She did not look at Grandfather as she replied. "That's right. Our fathers have known one another for decades. They met at Oxford, in fact."

"Ah, it must have been nice to know someone already when you arrived at university. Especially as you would have been one of the first groups of female students formally admitted to your college. If you don't mind me asking, what do you study?"

Her eyes flicked up to look at him then and I could see she

was considering whether to answer his question and what harm it could do her. "I study law and jurisprudence. I intend to become a barrister." She spoke with great poise, and it appeared that she'd chosen her career well.

Grandfather shifted in his low seat. "Is there any specific branch of the law that interests you?"

She failed to suppress a smile then. "Yes…" Her eyes darted away to the horizon. "Criminal."

"Oh, how fascinating. If there's anything I can do to help, please don't hesitate to ask. I know all sorts of people at the Inns of Court. Judges, barristers and several KCs."

She was clearly not moved by the offer, and I had to assume that her wealthy family held all the influence she required. Nevertheless, she nodded her thanks and waited for the next question.

When it came, it was a good one. "You were in love with Simon Cumberland. Is that why you killed him?" The kindly expression had vanished from my grandfather's face and a keen look replaced it.

"Whoever told you that?" A moment of tension followed her words.

Grandfather's virtuoso performance was undermined by the fact that he couldn't get comfortable in his chair and had to keep sitting back up as he slid down the canvas. It was actually quite funny, though I managed not to laugh.

"Nobody, but I saw the uncomfortable looks that your boyfriend was shooting him all day yesterday, heard the snide comments you directed his way and drew my own conclusions."

Perhaps her legal instincts kicked in, as she immediately set out to defend herself. "I have Rufus now, I don't need anyone else." Her eyes flicked towards the house as she spoke and, much like my grandfather, I knew she was lying.

"That's not the whole story, is it?" I don't know why I still haven't learnt to keep my mouth shut at moments such as this.

Grandfather didn't seem disturbed by my intervention and added a question of his own. "How long have you and Rufus been courting?"

She let out one of those snarling laughs that I'd seen her direct at her friends so often the previous evening. "My goodness! Courting? You do sound old fashioned."

"And you haven't answered my question."

She was entirely unphased by his snapdragon response. "Well, that's because I haven't the faintest idea how to respond." She threw her head back theatrically and released a tittering laugh up towards the clear blue sky. "There's no obvious name for what Rufus and I are enjoying. I haven't taken him home to my parents or put a notice in The Times. We simply attend dances together, go to the same parties with friends. It's never been particularly serious."

"Until today," I whispered and, in a split second, her eyes locked onto me.

"Possibly. And what of it?"

Normally, I would have crumbled under the pressure of an adult looking at me with such ferocity, let alone a pretty young lady. Perhaps it was thanks to my grandfather's training, but I knew that the best thing to do was smile and pretend it was of no importance.

"Oh, nothing. Nothing at all." I shook my head as though I'd said something foolish. "I'm just a bit of a romantic; I like it when two such nice people end up together."

I watched her melt at my innocent act. "You sound like your mawkish brother."

Grandfather gave me an appreciative wink while Hortensia wasn't looking, then took control of the conversation once more. Well, first he had to turn on his side a little to maintain his position in the slippery chair, but then he delivered his next challenge.

"Tell me more about Simon."

"Of course. What about him?" She reached into a small purse to extract a cigarette case, as though the question was of very little significance whatsoever.

"What was he like? Who do you think would have tried to tamper with his parachute?"

She took her time lighting a long French cigarette and didn't look up again until her lungs were full to the brim with smoke. "Simon was… Well, Simon was rich and handsome and really rather dull, but what can I say? When I first arrived at university, that's exactly how I liked my men. Anyway, that's all in the ancient past."

"You're really not much of a romantic, are you?" I suggested, and she shrugged her shoulders cheerfully.

"No, I'm being dreadfully unkind, which is why my friends

always tell me off. Simon was loyal and generous and could be good company. But he had a short temper and started fights far more often than any man should."

"You mean he got into physical brawls?" Grandfather's snow-white moustache drooped in surprise.

"Yes, isn't it shocking? A fine young man like Simon Cumberland with a channel of violence running just beneath the surface." She turned to me once more and directed her smoke past my face. "You must have seen the black eye he gave your brother last year?"

"Albert?" I sounded all squeaky, like a thirteen-year-old boy. Now that she mentioned it, I did recall him wearing mother's make-up a lot a few months prior, but I'd put it down to a phase he was going through. "He's no fighter."

"You're right there. They were arguing over Evie, of course. She loved it, but it got out of hand and poor Albie got a smack to the face. It was all over in seconds."

"So you think that my grandson killed Simon?"

"No, of course I don't." She stopped to extract a fibre of tobacco from between her teeth, then looked up at Grandfather again. "I think it was Evie."

CHAPTER NINE

"You don't have any evidence!" After hashing it out for five minutes, Lord Edgington was beginning to lose his temper.

"Fine, don't listen to me." Hortensia did not appear intimidated. "But I know my friends better than you ever could, and I'm telling you that she did it. It's the only thing that makes sense."

"But why would she have done it?" I asked, as I didn't want my grandfather slipping a disc from the stress.

"That's your job to work out, not mine. But I know what I know. Evangeline De Vere is not the angel everyone makes her out to be. Perhaps she got bored with poor Simon, or perhaps she did it for fun. Either way, she's the only one who would have cared enough to snip his line."

"How do you know that it was his line that was snipped if you weren't the one who did it?" I was quick to thunder back at her.

She was not intimidated. In fact, I was beginning to think that nothing could frighten her. "Because your idiot brother has been blabbing about it all morning."

"Typical Albert!" my grandfather and I muttered as one.

She rolled her eyes then in an over-the-top display of just how inconvenienced she was by our continued presence. I noticed that there was no sign of the tears that had previously plagued her.

She crossed her legs at the ankle rather affectedly. "Listen, I'll do a little summary for you to save us all time. One, I didn't kill Simon. Two, I don't know who did. Three… but I think it was probably Evie." She beamed up at us, as though she'd just solved the case.

Grandfather's temper was instantly triggered. "I don't believe you for one minute. I think you know more than you're saying and, if I'm being totally honest, I think that you killed Simon, because you didn't want your oldest friend and rival having him."

"Ha!" This sound she made was like an arrow from a bow. "The very idea is absurd."

"Is it? I'm sure that you would be more than capable of cutting a man's life away." It was rare that the old man responded in quite such a personal manner. "Maybe not with an axe to the head or a sword through the heart, but I have no doubt that someone like you could manage a simple snip of a rope. It probably didn't even feel like you were murdering him, did it?"

She didn't fall for his provocation, but put on a naïve expression and said, "And what sort of person do you think I am?"

I could tell how deeply Hortensia had got to him, but he managed to calm himself before delivering his final riposte. "A self-interested, calculating, stone-hearted woman who hasn't got a single good word to say about her own friends."

This would have been quite the parting shot if he hadn't struggled to extract himself from the deckchair. Instead, he had to roll from side to side like a seal. When that didn't work, he waved me over to help him up.

"That didn't go as I'd been hoping," he told me once we were out of earshot.

"Don't worry, Grandfather. She's a shrewd character. I think you played it just fine."

He ran one hand through his long grey hair and tried to compose himself. "I was the officer who secured the confession of the Dartford Butcher. I single-handedly fought off the Fenwick brothers with nothing but my cane and a pocket bible. I was recommended for three medals of bravery in the course of my career."

I felt I should probably interrupt, as he'd worked for the police for over forty years and would no doubt have gone on listing his accomplishments for some time. "Yes, but she's obviously a smart young lady and was trying to get under your skin."

He showed no sign of having heard me, but ground to a halt beneath the long, terraced walkway. "I don't trust her one bit."

Off in the distance, I spotted a car coming through the main gate to Cranley Hall. It was a shabby little Triumph two-seater which had once been black but now looked worn and dented, like a tin can that children have used in place of a football.

"Inspector Blunt is here," I said because he wasn't paying attention, and I had no doubt he was still reliving the conversation he'd just endured.

My announcement seemed to help him focus. He caught sight of the car and came back to himself. "We must speak to Evangeline before he comes to destroy the work we've done. This murder was carried out by an opportunistic coward. Little planning or thought went into it, and I will not be outfoxed by such a case. We'll hand the killer to Blunt and then have lunch on the terrace."

I could tell that this burst of bravado lacked his usual iron-clad confidence, but I didn't like to disagree. He entered the house through the petit salon and scouted along the west wing corridor in search of Evie.

In the end, we found her with my brother in the ballroom. The poor girl's eyes were still red and Albert was clearly doing all that he could to comfort her. They were standing in the middle of the room together, as though waiting for an orchestra to start the next dance.

I noticed that my grandfather paused on the threshold to watch them. Perhaps it was a flight of my own imagination, but I thought I might have some idea what he was thinking. Seeing those two young people ready for their dance, I couldn't help but recall what had happened at the spring ball just weeks earlier.

He cleared his throat softly. "Evangeline, I need you to come with me this minute."

She looked rather startled as she saw who was addressing her. "I... Yes, of course, Lord Edgington. Albie has already explained what happened. I'll do whatever I can to help."

My brother nodded his head at her and let go of her hand. They held one another's gaze like parting lovers, and I had to worry how long it would take Albert to get over his broken heart this time.

When Evie had almost reached us, Grandfather turned around and unceremoniously sped off down the corridor. "Sorry to be so abrupt," he bellowed without looking back, "but if we're not quick, the police will interrupt. I think it's in everyone's interest that we move quickly."

"Albert," I thought to shout back into the ballroom, "do what you can to slow down the inspector."

All the running around that grandfather had been doing had finally caught up with him and, halfway along the corridor, he had to pause to regain some strength. He was still the fittest seventy-five-year-old I'd ever met.

"Grandfather, where are we going?" I felt compelled to enquire when he started the race once again.

"One place where the police won't think to look for us." He would not say more than this and shuffled along at great speed in the direction of… I wasn't quite sure where.

Luckily, in her yellow floral summer dress and soft plimsolls, it was easy for Evie to keep up. In fact, I was the one who struggled most and might have confessed to killing Simon myself if it meant I could have a nice sit down in a prison cell.

"The kitchen!" my grandfather finally announced, as he led us down the servants' stairs.

"Well, you are most correct, Lord Edgington," Evie agreed. "The police won't think to look for us in here. I'm fairly confident that my parents don't know where the kitchen is in our house. My father has certainly never set foot in it."

"Not like his lordship then, Miss," our rather forward footman informed her, as he carried a box of deliveries towards the larder. "He often comes down here for a chat or a game of cards these days."

Grandfather looked a little embarrassed at this, but nodded his thanks to Halfpenny all the same. The kitchen was quite the hive of activity. Cook and two of the kitchen maids were busy preparing our lunch, my beloved Alice had come by with a message for Todd, and our Chauffeur himself was sitting in a corner reading a book – now that his duties guarding a dead body had concluded.

The master of the house ushered our final suspect over to the immense table where my family's food had been prepared for at least the last century.

"Would you like a cup of tea, M'Lord?" Cook asked before we could get started.

"No, thank you, Henrietta. I'm rather pressed for time and-"

"A whisky, M'Lord?" Halfpenny enquired. "We've just today had a delivery of a delicious double-"

"No, no." He was struggling with his temper again. "I'm absolutely fine. Just pretend we aren't here and I'll be out of your way in an instant."

"Actually, I'd rather like a tea after all that running about," I said without thinking, and Grandfather turned his gaze upon me.

"No, you wouldn't, Christopher."

I took his word for it and decided not to say anything else.

"Evangeline. I need you to tell me who might have wished Simon harm." There were no tricks or stratagems this time. He cut straight to what we needed to know. "I have learnt that both Chet and my grandson Albert…" He searched for the right word. "…pursued you at the same time as Simon. Do you think that either one of them could have been involved?"

She looked down self-consciously at her delicate hands. "I don't think so, M'Lord. Albert and Chet normally got along with Simon, despite the fact that they all…" She smiled then, but didn't finish the sentence, as it would have made her sound vain.

Grandfather's voice softened a little, as I sat down opposite them at the table. "I hope you don't find it uncouth to mention, but my wife was truly beautiful, just as you are, my dear. I had to fight off any number of suitors to win her heart and her hand and, when we were finally married, she told me something I would never have expected." He paused to collect his thoughts. "She said that her beauty was a burden, and she wished that she had been born as plain as any wallflower."

Evie was crying again before he'd finished the story. "That's why I chose Simon. It wasn't his wealth or his looks that made me feel so strongly for him, but the way he treated me. We only spent a short time together but, when we were alone – when it was just the two of us – he spoke as though he'd loved me his whole life. Albert, Rufus, Chet and all those other boys are sweet of course, but Simon truly loved me."

Cook had been hovering and now placed a plate of freshly made jam biscuits in front of Evie to make her feel better. "You have a good cry, Miss."

Grandfather gave her a disapproving look, and she scuttled back off towards the immense oven.

"What about Hortensia then?" he continued, when Evie had recovered somewhat. "You've known one another for a long time, and I couldn't help noticing the rivalry between you."

Drying her pretty brown eyes with the tips of her fingers, she looked up at the bronze pots hanging high on the wall. "Oh, yes. You're probably right. I've always tried to be kind to her, but I'm not sure that friends are a concept in which Horty greatly believes."

This was just what Grandfather wanted to hear, and he urged her to continue. "Very good. And I believe she had feelings for Simon, isn't that right?"

Evie's every emotion was there to read on her face, which she now crumpled in confusion. "But that was years ago. Back when we were first at university. And, even then, it was more first-term excitement than any kind of relationship. They might have sat in the dining hall together a couple of times, or been at the same parties, but I doubt either of them have thought about it since."

It was Grandfather's turn to show his emotion. He brought a fist down onto the solid block in front of us and forced the plate of biscuits to rattle. "I'm clutching at straws," he admitted. "Half an hour ago, it felt as though we were getting to the truth, but the longer I investigate, the less sure I am of anything."

"I wish I could help you more," she said and put one small, smooth hand on the old man's arm. Even in her grief, she was doing her best to comfort others.

As Grandfather had taught me – and I'd already forgotten time after time – you mustn't let sentiment get in the way of an investigation. I forced myself to say something that I'd rather not have.

"Hortensia told us that she believes you killed Simon." Her sobs grew louder, but I had to keep going. "Why would she think that?"

It took some time for Evie to respond. Her cheeks were glossed with tears and there was a small puddle forming on her lap. "She could only say such a thing because she's barely human. I've always known it, but that girl doesn't think like other people. In place of a heart she has a legal dictionary and instead of a soul she has a hanging judge's gavel." She had to stop then to pull more air down into her lungs. "How she could think that of me… I can't tell you."

I looked at my grandfather, but he was content to let me continue. "What if Hortensia wanted to hide her own guilt by pushing it on to you? What if she really was in love with Simon and couldn't bear to see the two of you together?"

She peered at me across the table, which was covered with large vegetables from the kitchen garden. When I left school the previous day, I had never expected to be interviewing a beautiful woman over a pile of fennel and broccoli.

"No, I've told you. I don't think that can be the case. I know that it's impossible to say what's really going on in another person's mind, but I've spent half my life with Horty, and she's simply not the sentimental type. That's part of the reason it's so odd to see her fall for

Rufus the way she has. And besides, if she really was so jealous, why did she kill Simon instead of me?"

The three of us fell into silent thought then. I could tell that my grandfather had pinned his hopes on some grand secret that Evangeline would reveal, but it wasn't to be. At least, not with Inspector Blunt already on our heels. We had all the evidence there was to find from the scene and we'd spoken to every last witness, but there was no clear path to identifying the killer.

"Thank you so much for trying," Evie continued when no one else had spoken. "The thought that Simon was murdered is still impossible for me to comprehend. From what I know of my friends, though, I really don't think any of them are capable of such a thing."

"You only met Chet this year, didn't you?" Grandfather tried one last time, but I could tell from the way he spoke that he didn't expect anything to come of it.

She took a bite of a biscuit, and it actually seemed to perk her up.

"Yes, you're right, of course. But you can tell that he's a good person. And the fact that Simon and I knew him less than our other friends surely reduces the chance that he's the killer."

Lord Edgington rose from the table and bowed gracefully to our witness. "Thank you for your patience with an old man, Evangeline. I imagine the police will wish to speak to you before long."

I joined him on my feet and she smiled sadly at us. "In which case, I might stay here for a few minutes longer with these lovely biscuits."

"You take all the time in the world, Miss," our cook shouted across the kitchen. She was an incorrigible eavesdropper, but it was hard to hold it against her.

My grandfather turned to leave, just as Alice arrived with a message. Such tasks would normally have fallen to our butler, but he was… well… otherwise engaged that weekend.

"The police are waiting to speak to you, M'Lord. That Inspector Blunt says it's urgent and he won't wait around for you any longer."

Grandfather nodded and I could see the sorrow it would cause him to hand over the investigation to his old rival, but we'd explored every avenue and come to the end of the road.

"Very, well," he grunted in reply and whistled for Delilah, who was in her usual spot by the hearth. "Christopher, it's time to go."

CHAPTER TEN

It was a solemn journey that we took back through the house. Having already made Evangeline cry, it was my moment to feel guilty for the pain my grandfather was now suffering.

"Perhaps we were too soft on her?" I suggested, as we climbed the stairs. "Perhaps her doe eyes, perfect skin, angelic smile and–" I stopped myself as I was getting carried away. "Perhaps she killed her boyfriend, knowing that we'd never suspect such an innocent-looking creature."

"No," he replied with great confidence. "If she wanted to get rid of him, she could have simply called off their relationship and been done with it. What possible motive would she have?"

"Then Rufus? It was his knife at the scene of the crime. The other evidence we found might just have been a coincidence; perhaps he really did drop the murder weapon."

He shook his head but didn't look at me as we slowly progressed along the hall. "He had over an hour when nobody was in the changing room. He could have retrieved the knife and none of us would have been any the wiser. The traces of Hortensia's bright red lipstick and Chet's hair blacking tell me one thing; the killer planted the evidence. That much is clear, but I don't know who did it and I don't know exactly why."

I'd run out of theories and left him to pour over his gloomy thoughts. Chet didn't seem like a savage murderer, despite his military past. Albert couldn't possibly have done it – or could he!? No, he couldn't. And we'd ruled out everyone else.

It truly was an unsolvable case.

"I've got it!" Grandfather suddenly yelled. "How did I fail to see it before?"

I had no idea what he was referring to, but assumed he'd read my mind again and went with, "So you think that Albert could be guilty after all?"

He stopped and looked at me as though I was a cucumber short of a cucumber salad. "No, of course not." He narrowed his eyes and moved closer, perhaps trying to ascertain whether I'd been drinking. "That's not the first time you've suggested your warm-hearted, light-headed brother could be a killer. I think you might have to talk to a specialist when this is all over."

I carefully moved the topic on, and we continued the trek down the hall. "So, what did you realise?"

He pulled his lips in tighter and would only say, "Not yet. There's someone I need to talk to first."

About three miles away, at the very end of the corridor, Inspector Blunt came into view. He was not happy to see us. "Edgington, your grandson has done nothing but obstruct this investigation. There's been a murder and I have every right to search this property."

Albert was trailing behind, looking sorry for himself. "I tried to tell him that he couldn't come in, Grandfather, but he simply wouldn't listen."

The conversation was carried out in excessively raised voices. It was Lord Edgington's turn to throw his down the hall – and deafen me in the process.

"Not to worry, my boy. Why don't you make the inspector a Pimm's cup and find him somewhere to sit in the sun and I'll be with you both in five minutes?"

I could see that the ever-grimy Inspector Blunt was feeling torn. "I am rather thirsty, I must say," he eventually muttered. "But stop trying to fob me off. I'm here to do a job and I will not be…"

We didn't hear anything more as we'd turned off the corridor to cut through the smoking room and out onto the terrace. Looking over the concrete balustrades, we could see Rufus and Hortensia lying entwined on the picnic blanket once more.

"Hortensia," Lord Edgington shouted down, "I need to speak to you this minute."

Blunt had gone through the ballroom and was out on the terrace by this point. "I said, you're not going to fob me off with a tasty drink."

Moving faster than I'd seen him all day, my grandfather headed towards the gardens, but took a moment to reveal his plan. "Chrissy, you'll have to intercept the dreadful man. I need two minutes alone with Hortensia, so keep the inspector busy."

I stopped in my tracks. "How am I supposed to do that?"

He didn't look back, but shouted his idea over his shoulder. "I don't know… Try fobbing him off with a tasty drink!"

He ploughed down the steps, collected Hortensia from the gravel path where she was waiting, and pulled her through the door to the changing rooms before Blunt could see where they'd gone.

"How did he...?" the inspector began, scratching his chin as he tried to process this disappearing act.

"Urmmm... how about that drink?" I gave it my best attempt.

I didn't actually have any of the materials required to make that delicious summer cocktail, so I had to call for Halfpenny, who was restocking the drinks room and came at a quick pace.

I got Blunt settled down at the table where we'd watched the sunset the night before. Chet appeared from inside the house, Rufus came up to see what the fuss was about and the Pimm's was almost ready when my grandfather marched Hortensia back out of the house and up the stairs.

"Blunt, I've got your murderer for you, right here."

CHAPTER ELEVEN

"I won't be having none of your theatricals, Edgington." The officer spat the words (and any amount of saliva) from his mouth as his rage frothed out of him. "If you don't hand over the killer in five minutes, I'll drag you down the station myself. There's only so many murders that can go on around here without us coming to look at the common thread; Lord High and Mighty Edgington himself."

To say that the two men had a troubled history was an understatement.

"I don't need five minutes," Grandfather replied. "I can do it in two. I've just put my case to my grandson's friend here, and she confirmed my theory."

I could see how much the completion of his task had soothed him. He pushed an extremely affronted Hortensia towards the table, and she sat down with a screech of cast-iron on concrete.

"What's going on?" Chet asked, his central European by way of New York accent once more coating every word. "Are you saying she killed Simon?"

"Wouldn't that be fun for you all?" our apparent culprit responded.

A small voice was heard at the far end of the terrace. I couldn't make out what it said, but turned to see Evie running towards us. Delilah sprang off to accompany our latecomer. It would have been rude not to wait for them, so grandfather bided his time and Blunt sipped his drink.

I watched the other members of our party as they suffered through the uncertainty. Chet and Rufus were clearly terrified that they were about to be outed as killers, but Albert looked oddly relaxed as he helped himself to a chunk of strawberry that Halfpenny had cut.

"What's happened? What are you all doing here?" Evie panted out as she arrived. Chet immediately gave up his seat and put a hand on her shoulder.

"Lord Edgington knows who the killer is," he told her gently.

"Well, the jury's out on that one, fella!" Blunt slurped at his drink and, as if on cue, two uniformed officers appeared from the house.

Ignoring his old rival's comment, Grandfather began his

explanation. "I knew it the moment that I discovered Simon had been murdered; this was not some long gestating plot, but a crime of fury and passion. We saw that his parachute was in good condition out on the lawn and could only have been tampered with in the fifteen minutes or so that it was left unattended in the changing room. You'd all been in that room, most of you alone, and so it was impossible to rule out any one of you."

He leaned over the table with his weight on his knuckles and slowly peered around the assembled figures. "And yet, there were a limited number of suspects who could have been involved and few clear motives for the poor man's death. My suspicions bounced from one of you to the next, without ever settling on the culprit until a few minutes ago."

"Get to the facts, Edgington. The clock's ticking." Despite his tough words, Blunt had just topped his Pimm's up with more lemonade and was swishing the fruit around in his glass.

"First the evidence." Grandfather did not appear intimidated by his crotchety colleague's words. "On Simon's parachute after we landed, we found stains where the line was housed. They were consistent with marks from shoe polish or, indeed, hair blacking." All eyes shot in Chet's direction. "I immediately considered this suspicious and, when I found a neat cut in the safety cord, the only possible conclusion was that Simon had been murdered."

He paused to let the reality of this simmer in his audience's minds. "My assistant Christopher and I came back here to examine the changing room before anyone else could tamper with the scene. We would discover several clues which were simply too obvious to accept at face value. There was a trace of deep red lipstick on the shirt that Simon had left behind, a golden-brown hair…"

"But I didn't-" Evie's voice shot up like a rocket before Grandfather silenced her with a look.

"…And last, but perhaps most importantly, a small pocket knife with the initials R.L.S. upon its handle."

Each person's gaze bounced around the group before, to a man, we came to focus on Rufus.

"I didn't do it," a scandalised tone squeaked out of him, and Grandfather must have realised how cruel he was being, as he quickly moved us on.

"It was too convenient an explanation, once again. Though I have no doubt that there are killers stupid enough to leave a monogrammed murder weapon at the scene of their crime, I can't imagine that any of you fit that description. It only made sense, therefore, that the evidence had been planted to incriminate Chet, Hortensia, Evangeline and Rufus." He left a pause for us to solve this particular conundrum. "Which would leave my grandson Albert as the likely killer."

My brother's face was instantly drained of colour and he took a step back from the two constables who were eager to arrest someone. He looked like he was about to sprint away.

"Don't be ridiculous, boy," Grandfather snapped. "Stay where you are and calm down for a moment."

Albert let out a hard-done-by moan and returned to his place.

"I initially had to consider whether Evangeline herself could have put my grandson up to the task. I've seen nothing from Miss De Vere all weekend but innocence and charm and, I must admit, that made me suspicious. After all, the single hair I found at the scene could easily have found its way on to her suitor's clothes without needing a scheming killer to place it there. Luckily for the pair of them, Evie is just as innocent as she seems, and I struggled to believe Albert had such violence in him."

My brother still looked anxious, but Grandfather either didn't notice or didn't care.

"I considered the motives of each of you. Rufus informed me of his devotion to Hortensia, and so I wondered whether he had attempted to get even with an old rival on her behalf. In fact, the tension that there clearly was between him and Simon led me to discover the feelings that Hortensia herself had once had for our victim. But this was just one of the wrong turns I would take on my path to the truth.

"Our pilot Chet, meanwhile, confessed to not being the person he claimed to be and to admiring Evie, as apparently all men in her surroundings must. I inferred from Hortensia that she and Evangeline, though friends from an early age, had always been rivals – whether in their families, their studies or, indeed, with the men who pursued them. But still, none of it added up."

He paused then, and a hint of his previous aggression rose to the surface. "I had evidence without foundation, theories with no link to

Simon himself, and enmity that did not appear connected to the crime. It was a puzzle with all the wrong pieces, and it left me confounded. I spoke to each of you in turn, racing to get to the truth before Inspector Blunt here could stake his claim to the case. And whilst my interviews gave me a picture of a group of young people whose rivalries and affections were tied up with one another's, I couldn't land on one clear solution."

His words died away, and silence gripped the scene. I looked at my grandfather and it was clear he was wracked with doubt and disappointment, which was compounded when Blunt started laughing.

"You don't know who the killer is, do you?" the crow-like inspector cawed. "All this talk and it still hasn't come to you."

Grandfather smiled, happy that Blunt had fallen for his trap. "I know exactly who the killer is, but it only became clear after I'd spoken to dear Evangeline. And, even then, the answer almost passed me by. You see, when interviewing various suspects in the same case, it is essential to compare, with forensic detail, the different versions of events. A good detective must lay each retelling on top of the others to determine the slightest difference. With the pressure I'd put myself under to identify the killer in such a short time, I'd missed a key discrepancy which told me everything I needed to know. There was one fact which I'd accepted at face value that not a single person confirmed."

He'd reeled us in like minnows, and no one dared make a sound. Peering around at each of the suspects, he took his time. "As soon as we discovered Simon's body, I told Christopher that beauty can be deadly, and this is one case where my initial hypothesis turned out to be true. There were three men who were obsessed with Evangeline; her beau Simon, my grandson and-"

"Hey, I was never obsessed with the girl." Our cool captain at last showed a flare of anger. "She's a good kid, but there are plenty of other girls in Oxford and I can cope with a broken heart just fine."

"Not you, Mr Novicki," Grandfather purred. "Not you, but your friend Master Rufus Longfellow-Slaughter." As much as he claimed to look down on showmanship, the old man couldn't resist a dramatic pause just then. "Rufus insisted that he'd been in love with Hortensia since they were first at university together, that he had pursued her only to be rejected, and yet no one else painted a picture of him as a lovesick devotee."

It was Hortensia who let out a stifled cry then; Rufus remained silent. His eyes were fixed on the horizon, his face passive, as Grandfather laid out the evidence against him.

"Evie mentioned that all the boys in the group had been sweet to her. Not just Albert, Chet and Simon, but all four of them. Rufus's whole defence was that he was smitten with Hortensia and so an unlikely culprit. He put on a show for us on the lawn, wooing the poor girl so that, when we discussed their relationship, she would make it sound as though they were sweethearts. And yet Rufus had eyes for Evangeline De Vere alone. He was the one who had played with Hortensia's feelings but never committed to her, not the other way around. I was right that Rufus was jealous of Simon, but not for the reason I assumed."

He looked out across the gardens as he considered his own words. "Perhaps I put the idea of murder in his head at dinner last night when I joked about my own parachute not opening. Wherever Rufus got the idea, it's safe to conclude that his argument with Simon pushed him over the edge and he seized his opportunity.

"Of course, you can't go about killing your friends without arousing suspicion, so Rufus struck upon a plan. He left his own knife at the scene, knowing that a killer would never do anything so foolish. But that wasn't enough. He thought that, by planting evidence against Chet and Hortensia, he could direct my attention to the man who had shown the most heartache and anguish over Simon and Evangeline's courtship. Had Albert been the killer, he obviously wouldn't have left any clue to point towards himself or his beloved."

"But the hair we found-" I began.

Grandfather turned momentarily to address me. "As I told you all along, it was just a hair. Evie had walked arm in arm with her paramour into the house, and so it made sense that we'd find some trace of her on his possessions. Rufus expected me to find every last piece of evidence and blame my own grandson. He thought that he'd chanced upon the perfect method to murder Simon without getting his hands dirty. With one slit of the knife, a promising young man's life was cut short." The retired superintendent leaned in closer to the murderer. "Or, two in fact, as you'll be off to gaol now, Rufus. And, for one reason or another, I very much doubt you'll be coming back out."

The boy who I had first taken to be a gentle, kind-hearted, badminton-loving sort of fellow, had changed before my eyes. Rufus still wouldn't look at us, even as the girls and Albert all sobbed. He tipped his head back to get the last tasty morsels of fruit from the bottom of his glass and rose to hand himself over to the police. The two constables stepped forward to place him in cuffs and a smile finally appeared on his face. It wouldn't stay there long.

"I would have loved you, Evie, with my heart, body and soul, but you didn't care. If you'd chosen me, none of this would have happened."

Lord Edgington did not sound impressed. "That is quite the least persuasive statement of love that I have ever heard."

I thought that one of the others would answer back to the monster before us. I thought they would scream, shout and swear, but no one did. With such anger ripping through Rufus, it was clear that whatever we said would only feed his hate. Inspector Blunt gave him a prod in the back to keep him quiet, and he was escorted to a waiting police car and out of our lives for good.

CHAPTER TWELVE

There was nothing that could salvage the once-happy weekend. We ate lunch together while we waited for Hortensia and Evangeline's parents to collect them. Chet didn't have such a luxury, but could stay at Cranley Hall for as long as he needed to recover from that dark day. Not even Cook's unique cuisine and some fine vintage wine could erase our sadness, and all attempts at conversation soon faded out.

Rufus was no genius. It had only taken my grandfather a couple of hours to worm out that rotter, and he still felt that the truth had evaded him for too long. Once Albert's friends had left, we retired to the old man's suite, and he collapsed into the armchair where he had spent so much of the last decade since my grandmother had died.

I could see that the morning had taken its toll on him, but he attempted to be cheerful for my sake. Ever his faithful companion, Delilah came to sit at his feet.

"I have to say, Grandfather," I began, as I landed in a chair on the other side of the window from him, "I was totally taken in by Rufus. I really thought he was heartbroken over Hortensia, and I felt so happy when it seemed that she'd finally accepted him. But it was the other way around all along. I feel quite guilty for the way we spoke to her now."

He looked up at the moulded ceiling for a moment before replying. "As do I, naturally. But that was a clever piece of theatre on Rufus's part, even if it did bring about his downfall. You see, he could disguise the relationship that the two of them had – he could claim to love Hortensia alone – but he couldn't influence what the others would say about him. It wasn't until we spoke to Evangeline that anyone mentioned he held feelings for her, but as soon as we knew that, the whole case looked different."

"I'm glad you caught him. And I'm terribly glad it wasn't Evie. Or Chet for that matter."

"Or your brother?" his eyebrows shot upwards and I could tell he was testing me.

"Of course! You know, I really rather like Albert and I didn't-"

"I know, Christopher." He relaxed into his chair and smiled at me. "I know."

I still didn't understand exactly how the old man had worked everything out, but I didn't want to look any stupider by asking more questions. We sat in silence for a few minutes, gazing out across the lake and the woods and that perfect sunny sky, until Grandfather spoke again.

"I hope you've learnt your lesson, Chrissy."

I very much doubted I had, but thought for a moment to consider. "Well, I'll never get my initials engraved on a murder weapon, if that's what you mean."

"Hmmm, that may be wise under the circumstances. But I was thinking more of the reasons behind the murder than the manner in which it happened."

I made a second attempt. "Is the lesson that we can always trust Albert to fall for the wrong girl?"

"No, not that either."

"Blacking your hair is a risky business?"

"Nice try, but no." I thought I might have one last stab at it, but he continued for me. "What I hoped you might land upon was that you should be careful who you love, Chrissy. Romance is not always the rose garden it first appears to be."

I considered his meaning before asking a question. "But you were happily married for decades, weren't you?"

He nodded slowly. "That's right."

"And you said that grandmother was the most beautiful woman you'd ever met."

"And?"

"Oh, nothing." I pretended that I was interested in a picture of hunting hounds on the wall above his escritoire. "I just wanted to check that not all pretty girls are dangerous."

His moustaches performed a happy little dance upon his lip. "No, of course they're not, Chrissy, but their entourage of admirers just might be." The immense glass and wooden grandfather clock in the corner struck four and my own grandfather smiled. "Time for afternoon tea, I think."

We'd only just had lunch, and I was pretty much stuffed, but I couldn't turn down one of Cook's salmon and strawberry sandwiches. Halfpenny soon arrived with a tray of treats and poured us both a cup of Earl Grey.

"Grandfather," I began with some hesitation, "it was rather overlooked with everything else that happened, but I think it needs to be said that I jumped out of a balloon today."

"I know, my boy. And I am very proud that you seized your opportunity."

"Does this mean that I'm..." Did I dare say the word? Yes, why not? "...brave?"

He laughed his baritone laugh. "Of course you are. Spectacularly so, in fact."

I let out a long breath. "That's a relief. It was actually quite nerve racking. I was entirely convinced that I was about to die."

He brought his cup to his lips but didn't drink. "Tell me, Christopher, would you do it again?"

I didn't have to think long to furnish him with an answer. "Nope, not a chance! I'm surprised I didn't have a heart attack."

The End (For Now...)

THE "LORD EDGINGTON INVESTIGATES" MYSTERIES

- **Murder at the Spring Ball**
- **Death From High Places** (free e-novella available exclusively at www.benedictbrown.net. Audiobook available at Amazon early 2022)
- **A Body at a Boarding School**
- **Death on a Summer's Day**
- **The Mystery of Mistletoe Hall**
- **The Tangled Treasure Trail** (Coming Spring 2022)

Check out the complete Lord Edgington Collection at **amazon**.

The First Lord Edgington audiobook, narrated by the actor George Blagden, is available now. The subsequent titles will follow in early 2022.

ABOUT THIS BOOK

Normally I have an interesting story to tell you about why I wrote a book, involving my family, ridiculous events from my past (like that time I got all moody and jumped out of a window to escape from some annoying people) and, most likely, my love of crime fiction. But with **"Death from High Places"** my main inspiration was, *aren't balloons pretty!!!*

Hot air balloons back then, weren't actually *hot air* balloons and the modern form we're used to now was developed in the middle of the twentieth century. It was great fun researching the hydrogen balloons they still used in the 1920s and the history of manned flight stretching back to DaVinci and the Montgolfier brothers, two French paper merchants who decided they wanted to fly. The failure and successes of the various other attempts between and around those famous figures is worthy of a book in itself. As is the history of parachuting, which I also had to spend a long time learning about. The knapsack parachute had just been invented by 1925 but people weren't jumping out of planes until a few years later.

"Lord Edgington Investigates…" is a mystery series, but it's also the story of a man crossing off items on his bucket list (a concept I can't mention in the book, of course, as it is very much a twenty-first century term). To complete all his wild plans, he needs his assistant with him, which means poor Christopher is going to have to do a lot of things he would never have imagined. And that brings us to the third main theme in these books, the relationship between a streetwise grandfather and his innocent grandson.

I think that you can see their relationship developing already in this novella and hope that you'll stick around to find out what happens in **"A Body at a Boarding School"** which follows this book!

THE "DEATH FROM HIGH PLACES" COCKTAIL

I have to admit that I'm not a massive drinker. I also have to admit that I love a good cocktail. Final admission, I prefer them sweet and fruity. When I was living in Barcelona, there was a bar around the corner from my flat which had cocktails for €2.50 all day. It was a truly dangerous place to visit and turned every screening of a Saturday afternoon football or rugby match into the start of something hedonistic.

Now that I am older and far soberer, there are only a few cocktails I drink with any frequency and a favourite is the Pimm's No.1 cup. It's a delicious, quintessentially British drink and, in the summer, is drunk everywhere from the Wimbledon tennis championship to my favourite music festival, Latitude in Suffolk. Garden parties at my mum's house wouldn't be the same without it and so I thought it was fitting that Chrissy should get to have a taste.

You can add more (or less) lemonade to suit your palate, but the fruit is essential and any remaining chunks are a tasty treat once your drink is drained. Here's the classic recipe…

A highball glass filled with ice
50ml PIMM'S No.1
150ml lemonade
Strawberry, orange & cucumber
A sprig of mint

Pimm's was first produced in 1823 in a London oyster bar owned by James Pimm. He sold a special gin-based drink containing a secret mixture of herbs and liqueurs served in a metal tankard (AKA a cup!) There are various cocktails that can be made with it (the Pimm's Royale with champagne is also delicious) and if you search online, you can buy it all over the world.

The idea for our cocktail pages was inspired by my friend and the "Lord Edgington Investigates…" official cocktail expert, Francois Monti. You can get his brilliant book "101 Cocktails to Try Before you Die" at Amazon…

ABOUT ME

Writing has always been my passion. It was my favourite half-an-hour a week at primary school, and I started on my first, truly abysmal book as a teenager. So it wasn't a difficult decision to study literature at university which led to a master's in Creative Writing.

I'm a Welsh-Irish-Englishman originally from **South London** but now living with my French/Spanish wife and presumably quite confused infant daughter in **Burgos**, a beautiful mediaeval city in the north of Spain. I write overlooking the Castilian countryside, trying not to be distracted by the vultures, hawks and red kites that fly past my window each day.

When Covid-19 hit in 2020, the language school where I worked as an English teacher closed down and I became a full-time writer. I have two murder mystery series. There are already seven books written in **"The Izzy Palmer Mysteries"** which is a more modern, zany take on the genre. I will continue to alternate releases between Izzy and Lord Edgington. I hope to release at least ten books in each series.

I previously spent years focusing on kids' books and wrote everything from fairy tales to environmental dystopian fantasies, right through to issue-based teen fiction. My book **"The Princess and The Peach"** was long-listed for the Chicken House prize in The Times and an American producer even talked about adapting it into a film. I'll be slowly publishing those books over the next year whenever we find the time.

Thank you all so much for being part of my club and in particular to my crack team, Joseph and Kathleen Martin, Esther Lamin and Clare and Bridget Hogg for helping with this novella. **"Murder at the Spring Ball"** is the first book in the **"Lord Edgington Investigates…"** series. There are several more novels already available and I'm working on the newest book now. If you feel like telling me what you think about Chrissy and his grandfather, my writing or the world at large, I'd love to hear from you, so feel free to get in touch via…

benedictbrown.net

Made in the USA
Las Vegas, NV
02 March 2022

44856599R00049